Samson H. Frost

Nights of Madness

© 2024 Samson H. Frost

Publisher: BoD · Books on Demand, Stockholm, Sweden
Print: Libri Plureos GmbH, Hamburg, Germany

ISBN: 978-91-8080-148-5

E A S T

I was at my brain-dead job, doing brain-dead tasks. The only highlight was that the clock was nearing 5 PM, so it was only 30 years to go. It was an office job. Papers to print and sign, customers to call, coffee to drink like the devil, and of course, ogling the female colleagues during breaks. That was my favorite time of the day, apart from sleeping. When I didn't have to be awake, that's when I truly lived.

I headed downtown. I only had an hour before the liquor store closed, so I was in a hurry. I hopped on bus 42. Damn if that dickhead Chester wasn't on the bus.
"Hey there," Chester said.
I reluctantly sat down next to him.
"So, you're out running errands?" Chester asked.
"Yeah, I have to get to the liquor store, they're closing soon," I said
"Right. Hey, I thought I'd have a few drinks myself today, maybe we could hang out?" Chester asked.

"Of course," I proclaimed, in stark contrast to how I really felt.

We got off the bus and headed towards the liquor store.

"Have I told you about my friend East?" Chester asked.

"No, who's that?" I said.

"He was at this liquor store last week, picking up some beers. The security guard grabbed him and asked if he'd been drinking," Chester said

"No kidding," I said

"Yeah, he had a little hair of the dog for breakfast, but nothing out of the ordinary. I swear, the security guards are getting power-hungry," Chester said.

"Damn straight," I said.

I picked out a whiskey and some beers. I didn't have a cent though, so Chester had to pay. I already owed him over a hundred bucks, but I justified it by my loathing of the guy.

Chester paid for us, and we headed towards the bus stop.

"Should we head over to Mary Beth's place?" Chester asked.

Mary Beth, an ugly old hag who had cheated death several times. They had to pump her stomach at the hospital at least once a week. No one knew how old she was, but rumor had it she was much younger than she looked. Apparently, she was married once. The guy had developed the payment systems for all the taxis in Slovakia, a real entrepreneur.

"Sure," I said, popping open a beer and downing it.

After an otherwise silent bus ride, Chester pressed the button.

"This is our stop," he said.

We got off, and I threw the empty bottle away.

"Pick that up," yelled some dad out with a stroller.

"Easy does it my guy," I said, as he flipped me off.

We arrived at Mary Beth's building and walked up to her apartment. Chester opened the door without knocking.

"Mary Beth? It's Chester," he said.

No answer. Chester and I looked at each other, trying to figure out our next move. We went into the kitchen, and Chester took a glass from the cupboard.

"Mary Beth!?" he called, pouring us each some whiskey.

I left Chester in the kitchen and walked around the apartment.

"Mary Beth, are you home?" I said.

The whole place reeked of shit and vomit. Stacks of boxes, newspapers, packaging, and other junk were scattered everywhere, not even the bathroom was spared. I saw spiders, beetles, all sorts of critters crawling around the mess. It was a goddamn ecosystem. I was about to open a window when the front door suddenly flew open.

"MARY BETH! WHERE ARE YOU, YOU FUCKING WHORE?" yelled someone who stormed into the hallway.

He had a leather vest, a white shirt, and light jeans. His clothes carried the memories of spilled drinks, greasy meals, and God knows what else.

"WHO THE HELL ARE YOU?" he said, pointing at me, "DID YOU FUCK MY MARY BETH?"

"N-no," I barely managed to say before a slap sent me crashing into a pile of books and other junk.

"Calm down, buddy," said Chester from the kitchen. "Have a drink."

He handed him a glass of whiskey. The guy in the leather vest grabbed the glass, downed it, and threw it at Chester.

"That whore, she's left me," he said.

"You'll find someone else, don't worry, buddy," Chester said.

I had gotten back on my feet. The chaos had knocked over a box, which turned out to be full of half-empty liquor bottles. I picked three up and handed one each to the leather vest and Chester. The leather vest went to the couch in the living room, kicked away the junk from it, and sat down. The former white couch was stained, and a sharp smell filled the room as the leather vest guy disturbed whatever the hell had settled on it. Chester sat down next to him; I chose to stand.

We started pouring it down our throats, bottle after bottle, beer after beer.

"We need some damn music," said the leather vest and turned on the TV. All he could find was static. He got pissed off and threw the remote out the window. The white noise at least provided some light as it started to get dark outside.

We drank and laughed heartily. Chester tried to stand on his hands but went flying into a heap of junk. The leather vest started laughing harshly, unable to control himself, beer spilling from his glass all over the room. He got up from the couch and walked to a corner of the room. He pulled out his cock and let a stream of piss whip a stack of newspapers.

"Have you heard about when Johnson went to the doctor?" he asked, looking over his shoulder at us.

"No, what happened?" Chester asked.

"'Mr. Johnson,' said the doctor, 'you must stop jerking off,'" said the leather vest and began to giggle, "'Ah fuck, why?' Johnson said. 'Well,' said the doctor, 'because I'm trying to examine you.'"

We all started laughing harshly. I pulled out three cigarettes from my pocket and handed them out.

"Damn, this is life, guys," said Chester, "we're living the dream now."

"Sure as hell we are," I and the leather vest agreed.

I had a soft spot for these damn gentlemen. Chester, well, he was my best pal—no two ways about it. We'd seen each other through thick and thin, and there was no better friend in the world. But that leather vest? He added something different to the mix. The guy had a presence, you know?

"Goddamnit, we need some fucking music," said the leather vest, and started singing.

"If today wasn't an endless highway, and tonight a wild and crooked path. If tomorrow didn't feel so endless, then loneliness is a word that doesn't exist," he sang, and I started crying.

I went to the bathroom, pushing junk away from the sink. I took a good long hard look at myself in the mirror.

"What are you looking at? Who are you to scrutinize me? HUH? YOU ARE NOTHING!" I screamed and smashed the mirror.

The leather vest kicked in the locked door. He punched me in the stomach, so I staggered backwards and lost my balance on some boxes. I flew up to my feet and aimed a blow at his ugly face. I missed and hit the shower wall, which came loose from its attachment to the ceiling. I flew into the bathtub, and he turned on the cold water.

"Cool off, kid," he said.

I shut off the water, stripped down to my underwear, and rejoined Chester and the leather vest.

"What's your name?" I asked.

"Call me Satan," the leather vest answered.

We kept drinking, cheering, singing, pissing on the floor and throwing things out the window before we all passed out.

Everywhere I looked it was barren, bare, dark. Dark mountains loomed in the distance, and around me was nothing but rock dust, gravel, and dirt. Suddenly, I heard a voice.

"You are the chosen one."

With a jolt, I woke up on Mary Beth's floor. That asshole Chester lay next to me, looking lifeless.

"Chester?" I said, giving him a nudge. "Chester, are you dead?"

"Uuh," he groaned.

I crawled up, shaking the beer cans, looking for leftovers. Not a trace of the leather vest, but the front door was open.

"Hey, Chester, I was thinking about something," I said.

"What, Hilding?" Chester said.

"Why do they call him East anyway?" I asked.

"Because he only jerks off to the east," Chester said.

KUMBAYA

I was still drunk when I woke up. It was something like Tuesday. "Kumbaya, my Lord, someone's crying" echoed in my ears, some song from the night before. What does kumbaya mean, I wondered, as Ingrid kicked the door open.

"What the hell are you sleeping in here for?" she said.

"What? Where am I sleeping?" I asked.

I looked around. I was on the floor surrounded by toys, a crib in the corner, yeah, I'd been here before. It was Ingrid's son Luke's room.

"Where's Luke?" I said, crawling to my feet.

"Where do you think?" Ingrid said.

I saw a pack of cigarettes on the floor and reached for one. I couldn't help but smile at the situation as I brought the cigarette to my mouth. Ingrid firmly slapped the cigarette out of my mouth, the hit jolting my awareness in an unpleasant way.

"Daycare?" I guessed.

Ingrid turned on her heel and walked off.

"You start in half an hour," I heard her say from the hallway.

I put on my finest clothes, which simply meant my least tattered ones. I eyed the ragged garments I had just thrown on the floor.

"What do you want, Hilding? What do you REALLY want?" I thought. "You don't know... you don't know... because you already have it." Dizzying thoughts that really did a number on me. I didn't know what they meant, so I ignored them and worked my way to the job.

I walked along familiar streets, humming that kumbaya song.

"Hilding?" I heard someone call. I saw a threatening figure crossing a lawn in my direction.

"I've got you now," he yelled.

I started jogging lightly. I realized it was Andrew chasing me. I had slept with his woman, and that was after borrowing money from him. Water under the bridge, I thought, but time doesn't heal all wounds, it seemed.

"Don't get all fired up now," I shouted.

Andrew was charging well, good bounce in his steps, maybe good shoes. But I was also a devil at running, fastest in my class in elementary school. After Josh, that damn nerd.

"I'm not the one who gave her chlamydia," I tried, but that only seemed to fire him up even more.

Thanks to the morning jog, I had five minutes to spare when I arrived at work. I'd managed to outrun him just in time. I didn't want that psychopath knowing where I spent my days. I walked into my office, sat down, and exhaled.

"What does kumbaya mean?" I wrote to Freeman.

I glanced at the clock and saw it was time for the morning meeting. Suddenly, anxiety took over. The hangover was creeping in. Kumbaya, I thought, trying to calm myself as I walked to the meeting room. People made noises at the meeting, but nothing seemed to mean anything. I was shaking all over, my head pounding. I noticed eyes were on me.

"What the hell are you staring at?" Keshani said. It hit me then that I was staring at women.

"Sorry," I said, immediately looking away.

"I stare at women," I thought, a welcome realization. "That's why," I thought.

Yeah, that's why everything went to hell for me, that must be it. If I stop staring at women, I'll be able to fuck like hell, I thought. This woman I'd been staring at now, a colleague, Keshani. She was beautiful. Maybe a bit too beautiful. It hurt to look at her, she was a symbol of the unattainable. Men lined up for women like her, and I didn't even have a ticket. I wonder how she fucks, I wonder *if* she fucks, I thought, when Keshani interrupted me.

"Shall we grab a coffee?" she asked, and I nodded.

Walking down the corridors to the break room, we met Kate. Here's the first woman I won't stare at, I thought, while looking down at the floor, up at the ceiling, anywhere Kate wasn't.

"Hi?" Kate said, puzzled.

"Well, hi!" I said, thinking it worked right away, she already wants me.

But she had a husband and kids, and taken women, I don't know. I'd tried that, and it rarely ended well. I should really move cities, there was so much hate in this one. I should move to a village in Africa where the women are naked. Maybe I'd get tired of the female body there and could live up to my full potential after that. I had something to offer, I knew it. I just didn't know exactly what. An old Buddhist monk once told me that the worst are more important than the best. The worst make everyone else feel a little less bad. I was doing all of humanity a big damn favor.

I knew there had to be something more than this. This carnal lust. All that crap. The alcohol, procrastination, depression. But I didn't know what, and the universe gave me no signs. It mostly pissed me off thinking about it. Spit it out already, for fuck's sake, what's the secret? What's the truth? The universe could give me a sense that there was something more but wouldn't give me the whole damn package. Anyway, I digress. Where were we? Actually, enough about me. Let's talk about you. You, reading this crap, what's wrong with you? Is this crap entertaining? Read something else, read Zen and the Art of Motorcycle Maintenance, or whatever it's called. Then you can explain it to me, because I felt dumber after reading it.
"Am I a dictionary you whore" Freeman replied.

THE PARIS MONKEY

Ingrid turned 30, and it was time for a hell of a party, even if it was the last thing I did. Mason was going to drive me and picked me up in a little red Ford. Mason handed me a beer as soon as I got in the car.

"Drink up!" he yelled.

Mason was an ex-boxer and soldier who made a living selling stolen goods. He was massive, benching 130 kilos. His beard was as massive as his body, and his hairline was solid. He was big, strong, and good-looking, he had everything I didn't.

I took the beer and downed it, because what the hell else was I supposed to do? Say no to Mason?

We went to the party. We drank beer and I listened to Mason's laments. His girlfriend had dumped him.

"I didn't even know you had a girlfriend?" I said.

"Yeah, we've been living together for the past 3 years," Mason said.

"Oh damn, sorry to hear that. Why'd she break up with you?" I asked.

"I don't know. She jerked me off, then she said it was over," Mason said.

"What did you do then?" I asked.

"I took my potted plant and went down to the pub," Mason said.

"I see... what kind of plant was it?" I asked.

"I don't know," Mason said.

"Well, what do you know?" I asked.

Mason didn't answer, and I didn't really give a damn.

There was free wine, and I had whiskey, I was in good hands. I cracked jokes, smiled, nodded, agreed, shared anecdotes, no one had anything on me. It felt like I'd won first prize in a contest I never entered. I met the love of my life, Sophie. I was on her like a bloodhound catching a scent, it wasn't like me, but hell, I was in love.

Later, at the pub, I saw Buckley's mother sitting at a table with a bunch of fat middle-aged men. It felt almost unsportsmanlike. She saw me, stood up, walked down the stairs towards the restrooms, glanced around, looking for me with her eyes. I followed her, she pulled me into the restrooms. She was wild, tearing apart the furnishings, clawing at me, like an animal.

"Fuck me," she screamed.

I fingered her, while we stood hugging and making out. Then she got up on the toilet seat and grabbed the backrest for balance, and I inserted it.

"How's Buckley?" I asked afterward.

"He's in the hospital actually, he fell off a rooftop, I don't know what he was messing around up there for...," she said.

"Sorry to hear that... send him my regards," I said.

"Eat my pussy, boy," she said.

"Hell no, that's disgusting, I just came there," I said.

I climbed the stairs from the restrooms, heading towards the dance floor. Sophie was dancing with some other guy, but I wasn't jealous. She was beautiful. She moved like a goddess, I knew of no one like her. I went to the dance floor, and Sophie danced her way to me. Everything was about us, everything was made for us that night.

The next day, I woke up naked on the floor. I crawled up, checked the clock, it was 9 AM. I was still drunk, wondering if it would ever end. I realized I was at a hotel, and that Sophie was sleeping on the bed. I sneaked down to breakfast, leaving Sophie to continue sleeping. I devoured that damn hotel breakfast like a madman, it was free for fuck's sake. But really, it wasn't free, no. I'd probably paid for this. And what little money I had came as a loan from my dear mother, goddamnit.

After breakfast, I jumped in the shower, had a notion that I could sing, but I couldn't. I finished my shower and crawled back into bed next to Sophie, who was still sleeping. She woke up shortly after. I kissed her, told her how beautiful she was when she slept, how much she meant to me, how nothing felt complete until I shared it with her. But she barely listened. She was sweating, sat up, and buried her face in her hands.

"What's wrong?" I asked.

"I dreamed about you, you were so cold," she said.

I sat up in bed, hugged her from behind, but she pulled away.

"I need some air," she said.

It felt like I'd done something wrong, but I laid back down, gave her space. I only met the damn woman last night. It was too many emotions in too short time for me, so I told her I'd swing by the liquor store to get out of there.

Everyone I met along the tired old road to the store greeted me, and I loved that town. I bought a bottle of whiskey, the kind that killed Dad, I wanted to test my luck.

I headed off to meet Frey and Ingrid. We were going to have coffee at a café. For some reason, I was hungry, so I bought lasagna. Ingrid talked about a newspaper article she read. It was about a monkey in Paris, that researchers had tried to get to paint something. After months of effort, they succeeded. The monkey produced the first drawing ever made by an animal. This drawing depicted the poor monkey's cage bars.

We went to a pub, and each had a beer, waiting for Freeman to arrive.

"My tooth hurts like hell," Ingrid said.

"What happened?" I asked.

"Some wisdom tooth acting up, I think," Ingrid said.

Her face looked swollen, one cheek bigger than the other.

"Better start drinking, it'll pass," Frey said, who always knew how to handle life's trials. He took a hefty gulp of his beer, as if to demonstrate.

Freeman stumbled in, already drunk. He was red as a tomato, something to do with blood pressure.

"Hey there!" he said.

"Where have you been?" Frey asked.

"I was going into the woods," Freeman said.

He went to buy a beer and then sat down at our table.

"I'm starting to feel ready to come out now," Freeman said. "I've been isolating myself since I quit drinking," he continued.

"You've been drinking six days a week," I said.

"Yeah, but I haven't had fun," Freeman said.

We went to a nightclub where we met Sophie. We didn't stay long; I was tired of the whole scene. A sense of hopelessness settled over me like a wet blanket. I just wanted to be with Sophie, not out among all these drunks. Sophie had bought drinks—whisky, beer, all sorts at the bar—and I can't say I blamed her. She had poor balance, so I had to hold her and guide her to the subway. On the train, she was completely out of it, leaning against my shoulder like a boxer after 12 rounds.

THE ORACLE

They threw us out into the night, and like stinking, filthy cockroaches, we scattered in every damn direction. My only friend from the lockup and I settled under a streetlight. He told his prophecies, like the Oracle of Delphi. If the Oracle had been a wine drunk. We were attacked by mosquitoes, and the Oracle killed a thousand, but to what avail? He handed out death sentences with his rough, sore worker's hands. Hands that had seen too much, for too long. I didn't kill any; I'm more for a good clean fight, live and let live, that whole bit.

The Oracle had found true love, the kind of love you should never stand in the way of. The jailer had a soft spot for the Oracle; she gave him Pasta Alfredo with tomato sauce. There's no tomato sauce in Alfredo, I said, but it was her own red sauce, the one from her crotch, if you know what I mean. The Oracle mixed a cocktail that could kill a horse, but a drink is a drink. Then we wandered along Greece's pitch-black streets.

Are you afraid of death, I asked. Death is simple; it's life that's a bitch, said the Oracle. The vultures circled above us, like an omen of where the night could lead if we weren't careful. We threw stones at them and the moon, and then it wasn't our problem anymore. Screw the stones, they know where they're going. The jailer said the Oracle reminded her of her aunt's dog, but no dog on this planet can mix a cocktail like the Oracle can.

We hit a crowded pub full of Greek sailors, mechanics, construction workers. We drank as if it was the last time we would drink in our lives.

"Have I ever told you about the time I almost became a monk?" the Oracle said.

"Nope, but I can tell it didn't work out," I said.

"Figured the robes wouldn't suit me," said the Oracle.

"What suits you?" I asked.

"This," said the Oracle, and as I let the chaotic Greek chatter wash over me, I think I understood.

We got out of the pub and stole a car and head straight for the border or hell, whichever came first. I have to tell him soon, I thought, the Oracle has the right to know, for God's sake.

"Almost there," the Oracle said after hours of driving, barely containing his excitement.

I mulled over how to say it. It's like ripping off a band-aid, just do it.

"Finally! I need to get out of this car…," I said.

The Oracle needed a beer, so we pulled into a gas station.

"Hey, by the way, there's something I have to tell you," I said.

"Yeah? what is it?" said the Oracle.

"I don't know how to say this but…," I hesitated.

"You know I love you, buddy, you can tell me anything," the Oracle reassured.

"You know what? Let's get the beers first," I evaded.

We went into the station and bought ourselves some cheap beers. They tasted awful, like it had been sitting out in the sun for three days, but it did the job. Then we hit the road again.

"Do you know what I love about you, Hilding?" the Oracle said.

"No, tell me," I said.

"You are one with Tao. You just live life according to the flow of the universe. How do you do it?" said the Oracle.

"I really don't. I have problems, big problems," I said.

Our conversation was interrupted. Neither one of us saw it coming. Just a slippery spot, and we found ourselves in the air just off the roadside. It was a long way down the slope. We flew around in the car like two pinballs, thrown back and forth. My head acquainted itself with every inch of the interior. Metal crushed, glass shattered, and it was as if time slowed down to a painful eternity. A surreal, gritty dream where you can't wake up. The adrenaline, the panic. We were in deep shit, and every thud, every sound, every moment whispered of doom.

I crawled out of the metal carcass that had just been a car.

"ARE WE ALIVE?" I screamed,

"I am alive," I heard from inside the wreck.

I crawled around to the other side and saw the Oracle still lying in the driver's seat.

"Are you hurt?" I wondered.

"I don't know, I'm afraid to check," the Oracle said.

He started coughing up blood.

"Have I punctured a lung," the Oracle said.

I called the emergency services.

"Hurry the hell up!" I shouted to the operator.

"This is a horrible way to die," the Oracle whispered.

I realized I had to say it now, otherwise it could be too late.

"By the way buddy. I almost forgot, you know the jailer, well, we've fucked."

ENCOUNTERS

Like a king, he stepped off the plane. People cheered. People wanted autographs. People were going crazy. The flight attendants had offered themselves up in the air. The booze and beer were free. I was going to meet him at airport. I had the wine, and that was what was needed to seal the deal for the evening. The time was just after 5 PM. Perfect timing. I sat on the train, sipping wine. I had three bottles with me, and a bottle of rum. The train pulled in, and I smacked into the door while getting off, like some clumsy old fool. The bright lights were messing with my head, so I put on my sunglasses. I went up to the gate. Freeman had passed out on a bench.

Calvin was sitting beside him, editing some tiresome pictures of girls. He worked with something related to that. Working 9-5 Monday to Friday, then you die, yeah great fun living, working all the time. Retire worn out, needing a machine to get out of bed, some old hag from home care swiping your money.

Tonight though, it was girls, beers, and wine for Calvin. He had rotted in loneliness lately. The girls threw themselves at repulsive men, savages, beasts, instead of Calvin, the superior gentleman.

We drank beer and we drank liquor. Then we went out into the night. An IT consultant invited us to an after-party. The three of us took a taxi there, the IT consultant paid. I expected suit-clad, high-intellectual, boring, well-groomed aristocrats, but was met by junkies and hippies. Someone was lying on the hallway floor, pointing at a shoe.

"He's taken LSD," said a long-haired, poncho-clad guy who looked like he hadn't eaten in months.

I noticed a very modern guy, he had really taken it to the extreme. He almost looked like a waiter, white shirt and a thin black leather vest over it. He stood trendily, spoke trendily, gesticulated intensely and French-like, yes, he was trend personified. The room consisted of two levels. The guy stood with one foot on each level, like some kind of king. He exuded confidence. He drank beer from a wine glass and held the glass with the stem between his middle and ring finger. I studied him for quite some time.

"Why do you look like that?" I asked.

"Why do you look like that?" he asked.

"I'm just messing with you; I love all people. May all people be healthy, happy, and peaceful," I said and hit him in the face.

The next day I woke up around 7 AM. I checked my phone, nothing from her, the one that got away. Instead, two missed calls from an unknown number, annoyingly similar to hers. A woman I hadn't seen in three years. Whatever, who the hell cares. Time to get out of bed, another fresh day to get pissed on. Sick, cold, alone, freezing.

With morning chores out of the way, I'd been awake for half an hour. I was already restless like a damn animal. Strange, why did she call me? She removed me from Facebook ages ago. I'd rather take a "you're a damn pig" to the face than getting removed as friend from Facebook. Maybe that's what I was going to get, a definitive end to an already completed chapter. Feels a bit too ambitious. Some women have signed up on Facebook just to add me and then remove me. But I don't have a big ego, I know I'm a little piss ant in the universe, my birth or death makes no difference, but this is my story, not the world's.

I met up Freeman and Calvin at a snowmobile party, whatever the hell that is. Calvin was a wreck. He'd woken up with his pants on, but not his underwear. Now he had both, as far as I know.

Some diligent company's snowmobile club organized the party. I wasn't invited or welcome, but I was present. Only half the snowmobile club was here, the rest were in the slammer. They all looked like Vikings. If you did genealogy on these animals, those are the kind of family ties you'd find. Calvin rummaged through the fridge in a storage room. He grabbed as many beers as his pockets could carry. I was scared shitless.

We decided to swap the Vikings for suit-wearing psychopaths instead. We headed to this town's only club. Worthless as such, expensive entry, rude bouncers, you name it. They seemed to think they were doing me a favor by organizing the madness. They didn't treat me as a customer, they treated me like a creep who deserved the electric chair.

The bartender pissed in a glass and gave it to me for ten bucks and then I went around looking for Freeman. It was full of animals everywhere, horny animals that wanted to fuck, me one of them, the biggest animal of them all.

I found Freeman at the beer, where I was buying some drink.

"Is that a mojito?" I wondered.

"No, it's not a mojito," Freeman said.

"Do you drink mojitos, Freeman?" someone shouted from the crowd.

"Shut the fuck up…," Freeman said.

"You sound sick, Freeman?" some woman he knew said.

"Yeah...," Freeman said.

"Can't you make me sick too? So, I can take sick leave," she said.

"Yeah, I'll make you sick. With chlamydia," Freeman said.

We moved towards the dance floor. Up front, we had the suit-wearing psychopaths and Calvin. He was shaking his hairy ass like there was no tomorrow. Drunk as a damn animal. The psychopaths were probably sober, who's to say? A bunch of cocksuckers.

A girl invited us to an after-party, everyone will be there, she said. She and I went ahead. Once there, time passed but not a soul showed up. I called Freeman.

"What? I'm at home sleeping," he said.

I had been tricked. She stared at me, like a psychopath. Did she want to kill me? I excused myself,

"I think I need to puke," I said and put on my jacket.

"Why don't you puke in the toilet?" she asked.

"No, I need some air too," I said

"Okay, but walk a bit, so the neighbors don't see you," she said.

Sure, I'll do that. All the damn way to the bus, then I'll go home.

A few days later, Freeman met this woman on a bus. He had taken a hit from a homophobe. Not that Freeman was gay. That detail was unnecessary, I guess. She turned out to be very kind and nice. Genuine and decent. Ugly as hell though. Not my words.

BEAR

I sat in the hallway, tying my shoes.

"Where the hell are you going?" Sophie said, like a broken damn record.

"Goodbye, we'll never see each other again," I said.

I reached for my jacket. Her little mutt came charging and barking. I grabbed the broom and swatted the little bastard away.

"By the way," I said, "you need to get checked, I have chlamydia."

I walked out, she screamed something after me, but I didn't bother to listen. I slammed the door behind me. After the echo of the slam faded in the stairwell, it finally got a bit quiet. After descending the three flights of stairs, I realized I had forgotten the car keys, so I had to trudge back up to the apartment. I yanked the door open, and a whiskey bottle came flying at me. I caught it, grabbed the car keys, and slammed the door again.

I jumped into the car that would take me far the hell away from there. Where should I go? I took a swig of whiskey. I longed for the forest. To move out into some damn tent or build a cabin with my bare hands. That would be something. It's so damn cold where I live. Maybe I should head south, southwest, inland. Sit and meditate, even though I don't have the patience for it, and try to find food and stuff. I couldn't hunt any animals, of course, I don't want to kill anything. Yeah, I wouldn't survive long in the forest. If I made it through the first week, I'd be well pleased. What a damn experience, stranded in some damn forest. Forget the internet, there's not even running water.

I pulled into the store to buy some beer. I paused by the tools. I wondered what one might need out there in the forest. A saw is probably a must, I thought, then moved on to the beer. I paid and went back to the car, threw the beer in the back, and drove off. I parked in our spot, took the beer, went to our entrance, and climbed the five flights of stairs to our apartment.

"Already back?" Sophie grinned.

I stormed past her, into the kitchen. I grabbed the coffee pot and poured a cup, which I practically downed. I dug out the Bluetooth speaker from the kitchen drawer and turned on some music.

"Turn off the music, I have a headache," Sophie bellowed.

I turned it up and moved with the music. I closed my eyes as I spun around on the kitchen floor. I was at a beach bar somewhere where the sun was shining, and the women were beautiful when Sophie made herself known again.

"TURN IT DOWN, I SAID, YOU'LL WAKE BEAR!"

With my eyes still closed, I yelled at her:

"DAMN WOMAN, SHUT THE HELL UP. DID YOU TAKE THE LAST COFFEE?"

I opened my eyes and grabbed the speaker. I hurled it against the wall, shattering it to pieces. Bear came running, attacking me again. I grabbed the damn mutt and tossed it onto the couch.

"Are you happy now, you witch?" I said.

I stormed out of the kitchen. I felt the tears welling up in my eyes. I loved that speaker; it was my best friend in the household.

I went into the office and slammed the door behind me, then sat down in the office chair in front of the computer. I rested my face in my hands and let the tears flow. Suddenly, the office door flew open, and Sophie stormed in.

"Let's make peace and fuck," she said.

"You don't decide that, now we drink," I said.

The doorbell rang. Outside stood two neighbors who had heard the commotion.

"Is everything okay in here?" they asked.

"It's fine, guys, this is how adults argue," I said.

We danced in the living room and made love to each other. Life was good, and I could hardly wait to see what tomorrow had in store for me.

JUST A FLUKE

I sat in the break room. There was this guy, Warren. He was well educated. But he dragged out his stories so damn long, he never got to the point. He spoke like a professor but lacked that crucial ability to disappear into himself and forget the audience. He spoke to be liked, not to express personal truths, and he did a poor job.

Warren was talking about punishments in school, and he was probably against it, but I wasn't listening. I thought about sex. All the time, sex, in one form or another. That's all this damn brain thinks about. Except when it gets it. Then it doesn't want it.

"Are you going to the party tonight?" Lydia asked.

"I think I'll go," Warren said.

"Count me in," I said.

There was going to be a party for all employees, and most everyone had signed up. The company had gone all out, bought loads of alcohol, and there was going to be an open bar. It could only go to hell, and I wasn't going to miss it. By the way, there will be some swearing in this book, so if you have a problem with bad words in a book, you should read the one about Zen and motorcycles instead.

Buckley put his arm around my shoulder and pulled me closer.

"Tonight, I'm going to get girls. Tonight, I'm going to eat pussy," Buckley said.

"Anyone in particular?" I asked.

"Before 11, I've got Peach. You'll see," Buckley said.

" I believe you," I said.

Evening came and with it the party. I heard Buckley was looking for me, but I always avoided him. He was one of those smug bastards who thought his opinions mattered to everyone else. Nothing really mattered, and we were all just going to die, but he hadn't realized that.

"Buckley is looking for you," Jodie said.

"Fuck off," I said.

Warren, who looked quite drunk, launched into his long-winded spiel. This time, though, I pricked up my ears.

"Imagine being gang-raped in the ass by a bunch of brusque guys," he said, not addressing anyone in particular at the table.

"Okay," I said.

"I don't mean you should worry about it happening. I mean, imagine it happened yesterday and today you're sitting here. Do you think those damn words you've underlined in your books and bibles would help you then?" Warren said.

Jodie and Lydia looked a little disgusted. He had a damn good point, though.

"Because it can happen, trust me. It can happen," Warren continued.

Anything can happen at any time, that's both the ugly and the beautiful thing about this strange life.

I went to the bar for a new beer. Buckley was there too, and I glanced at the clock. It read 11:08 PM, so I asked Buckley,

"How did it go with Peach?"

"Shut up, Hilding, I'm going to kill you. It's lights out for you," he said and lunged at me.

He was a heavy piece, but I managed to use his own momentum and spin him over the bar. He flew to the floor on the other side, screaming like a pig. I grabbed my beer and walked back to our table. Lydia and the gang looked at me wide-eyed, and I had never felt so close to getting laid. It had been weeks since last time. I was like a shipwrecked sailor, and the women around me were land far away in the horizon.

"You have something tormented in your eyes," Warren said.

"What should I say to that?" I wondered.

"Are you tormented?" Warren asked.

"No more than usual or anyone else," I said.

"We men need to start talking about feelings," Warren said.

"Yeah, but not tonight," I said.

"Get some grass, we have a donkey in the room," Warren said, and I couldn't take him anymore, so I left the table. I went to the bathroom and cried, like a real man.

It was time to wrap things up. Some of us headed downtown. A fancy hotel bar with dim lighting and expensive beers. I ended up next to Rachel. I spun a few tales that she seemed to appreciate, but I was also very tired. I kept at the beer, but it wasn't working for me anymore.

"Sorry, I need to go home now," I said, almost slurring from exhaustion.

I worked my way to the night bus that would take me home when I got a text from Rachel.

"Do you really have to go home?" she asked.

She was a good woman, slim and nice, but her message somehow bothered me.

Let me try to explain. I'm not well. I haven't been well for a while. I'm so damn tired. In a soul-crushing way. Tired of going through all this, of nothing ever getting resolved. You see, I have this pain, chronic damn pain, physical pain, in my back and neck. That's also why what Warren said spoke to me, the illiterate bastard. That gang-rape thing. You never know what's going to happen, suddenly you wake up one morning and you're in pain, and it never goes away. There are no underlined words in your favorite Bible that can help you then. There are no words on this earth that can help you. So, what's the point? I don't know, I just know that I'm depressed. So, I try to find my way back to that time when I could smile a genuine smile. When I'm drunk, I feel good. But it doesn't work to drink every day, trust me, I've tried. It works for a month, then the boss catches on, or your face gets swollen, and that's not a good look. I'm disillusioned and I miss the time when I could live in the illusion that everything is fine and dandy. But I'm constantly tormented by what my brain demands of me. Why can't it just shut up? I mean, it's ruining itself. The whole construct is a shoddy job, or maybe I'm too dumb to see the bigger picture. What do I even mean when I say "I"? What is "I"? I used to fool myself into thinking I understood these things, but now they're driving me insane.

So, Rachel wanted me to stay, but I wanted to go home. Therein lay my dilemma. I really wanted to go to Rachel's, have a beer and tell her everything I thought I knew about life. But at the same time, I saw no point in it. I might as well go home and blow my brains out on the balcony, like a real man. Alas, I went to Rachel's instead.

"Welcome," Rachel said as we stepped through her front door. It was cozily decorated in that way only women seem to pull off. A lamp here, a knick-knack there, I don't even know how to describe it. I lived in a bare and dirty 30-square-meter apartment, with windows the sun never really managed to penetrate. What do I know about decor?

It smelled like woman, and it made me happy. It had been a long time since I'd felt that scent. I mean perfume or something, not lower abdomen, though that smells good too. I grabbed a beer from the fridge and plopped down on the couch. Rachel was already there. She looked happy and agog, and I missed the time when I could feel those sorts of feelings.

"So, this is where you live," I said.

"This is where I live," Rachel replied.

I took a sip of my beer and inspected my surroundings. The living room had two large windows overlooking a natural area. It was dark outside, but you could still make out the shades of gold and red among the trees' autumn leaves. The trees swayed in the wind, and I knew I was lousy at life.

"What do you see?" Rachel asked.

"The trees. They're nice," I said.

"Or is it yourself you're seeing?" Rachel said.

"What do you mean?" I asked.

"When you see the tree, it creates something within you, and really that's what you're seeing, not the tree," Rachel said.

"Are you Dalai Lama or something?" I said.

"That's how it is with everything you see, really you're seeing yourself. You are everything," Rachel said.

"That's just crazy notions. Your ideas about life will be the noose you dangle from," I said.

Rachel sank into thought, and after a while she said,

"Why are you so bitter, Hilding?"

"Why aren't you bitter?" I said.

"Or forget that question, as if you knew why you're not. As if it were up to you. It's just a damn fluke that you're not. Everything is just a ruthless fluke," I continued.

Rachel went quiet again. I felt uncomfortable and weighed down by guilt. There was no reason to drag Rachel into my dark world. I decided to try and lighten the mood.

"Hey, want to sit on my face?" I said.

Rachel didn't answer, and I had just enough time to think I'd put my foot in it, before she stood up and gave me a light push that landed me flat on my back on the couch. She took off her panties under her skirt and sat straddling my chest. Then she moved up, and I got her magnificent genitalia over my mouth, and now it smelled lower abdomen.

EAT THE CAKE

I was in love with an amazing, wonderful woman. Blonde, short, and sweet—no, beautiful. But it was hopeless. I just had to face it. She didn't want me, not now, not ever. She was in love with someone else. I was sad for a day, then moved on. Met another. She didn't want me either. But this woman, the first one, we had history. When we laughed, we looked at each other. You know, in a group, the one you look at first when you laugh is the one you care about the most. Maybe she liked me a little, I often thought. She never looked at me with disgust, like other women. And what a body.

I was home, sober, on a Saturday. Calvin and Freeman were at the pub, going bananas. They bombarded me with texts and calls. But when I've made up my mind, I've made up my mind. Why was I sober? I don't remember, seems strange in retrospect. Maybe it was God tricking me. Because that very night, I got a text from this fantastic creature. She was crazy if she liked me, but she did, she must have. She wondered if I was out drinking wine, spirits, beer, gin and tonic, White Russian, all the usual. But instead, I was sleeping.

At seven in the morning, I was out driving the Granada. That was indecent, seven in the morning. Next to me sat the beautiful blonde goddess, better than all of us together. I picked her up from the after-party. I studied her while driving. She thought I was creepy. Then I saw it, a damn hipster. Out walking his little mutt. It was absurd, seven in the morning?! Obscene, damn it, that he had changed into his hipster clothes so early. Not a little cheeky. I braked.
"Roll down the damn window, let me talk to him."

She suggested we eat ice cream and go to her place. I hadn't been with a woman for a while, but I would have gone there anyway. I bought two ice creams for 2 bucks at the store, then we went to her place. I put the ice cream in the freezer. I asked about yesterday. Apparently, she had gotten quite tipsy. We chatted for a while, watched TV. I started getting sleepy, so I thought I had to take my shot soon.
"What did you want when you texted yesterday?" I asked.
"I don't know...," she said.
"Did you want me to come over and sleep here?" I asked.
"Maybe...," she said.
"Did you want sex?" I asked.
"I don't know what I wanted...," she said
"Do you want sex now?" I asked.
"Is that the only reason you came? To get some?" she said.
"No, no, I came because you wanted ice cream, it's in the freezer by the way." I said
Then she was sulky, then she started touching me, and I touched her, and then I kissed her and you know all the rest. It was a good day. The next day, I had anxiety. I called her.

"I never want to be something you regret, I have and always will love you."

"This is not our time," she said.

She once told me, "Hilding, you're an idiot."

"Oh... you sound like my mom," I said.

"Hilding," she said, "the animals don't care, the animals don't give a damn."

Okay, it wasn't her who said that I just realized. She hasn't said anything to me for a while. In fact, she's been avoiding me lately. But that's how it is. The animals, they roam around the forest, screwing and shitting, and they don't care. They leave the mama animals to take care of the kids, and that's not okay.

They say you can't have the cake and eat it too, so I tell you here and now, if you're presented with the cake, just eat it, damn it. There's nothing to save. Save a cake? There will be more cakes. Eat it, damn it. Eat like there's no tomorrow, because who knows, maybe there isn't? You can die, some dam can break causing a tsunami, and you can die. You don't even have a car. Can you get out of here? Yeah, so think about it, eat the cake, for fuck's sake, eat it.

CLEANING DAY

Freeman put the key in the lock and turned it. A chaos of clothes, books, teacups, contact lenses, wine bottles, liquor bottles, trash attacked all my senses.

"It's a bit messy," he said.

Centered in the room stood a table covered with stacks of books, the pages yellowed by time and cigarette smoke. In the corner lay a mattress, and on the mattress lay a woman who looked to be at least 60 years old. Freeman looked at her with a mix of irritation and compassion.

"Daisy Mae, wake up for heaven's sake," he said, lighting a cigarette.

"Daisy Mae!" he lightly kicked her legs.

She came to life and slurred something with a rough, almost animalistic, whiskey voice. I saw a pair of garters peeking out from under her skirt, and my cock didn't know how to react.

"You have to go, Daisy Mae," he said softly but firmly. "This is not the right place for you."

She crawled up, passed me and Freeman, and went into the bathroom. A sharp smell of urine shadowed her. I saw a small stain on the mattress.

"Is that my mattress?" I asked

"Yeah, my boy," Freeman said.

"Is that piss?" I asked.

Freeman turned the mattress over.

"You know what, it's probably just a little wine," he said.

Freeman put on What Is Love by Haddaway and opened a bottle of wine. I opened a beer, and we heard Daisy Mae vomiting in the bathroom. Then, with unsteady steps, she left the apartment.

"Alright, let's get started," I said.

I was there to help him clean up the place before he moved out. Seeing the mess made me change my mind. I needed the money though.

First on the agenda was the bathroom sink. Something had been blocking the flow there since a couple of weeks. Freeman unscrewed the water trap. The whole pipe was clogged.

"What the hell is that?" I said. The stench was brutal.

"It looks like algae bloom," said Freeman.

"Do you have baking soda?" I asked.

"No," said Freeman.

"Baking powder?" I said.

"No," said Freeman.

"Chlorine?" I said.

"No," said Freeman.

"Anything corrosive at all?" I said.

"No, who the hell am I, Martha Stewart?" said Freeman.

Freeman suggested we have a beer before we really dedicated ourselves to cleaning. Three hours passed in a flash.

"I've pissed in the sink a few times, could that be it?" wondered Freeman.

"Nah. I've also pissed in the sink once or twice," I said.

We had another beer each; it was nice to chat a bit. I don't know how many we had by then, but the table was cluttered with empty cans.

"So, are you seeing anyone?" Freeman wondered.

"No, you?" I said.

"No, what the hell do I know about love. I tried some online dating anyway. Between you and me, it's just a bunch of fatties," said Freeman.

"Really?" I said.

Freeman fetched two new beers from the fridge. I wasn't an idiot, I knew the cleaning wasn't going to happen anytime soon, but why should I care? I don't give a damn about anything.

"Have you seen Master and Commander?" he asked.

"The one with Russell Crowe?" I said.

"Yes, damn fine movie. When he jumps in the water, killing himself. They think he's Jonah or something," said Freeman.

"I thought it was slow. They're on a ship for two damn hours," I said.

"Shut up, it's a tragic damn story, I say." Freeman's voice was about to crack. 'It's a damn touching story,' he continued.

"It's absolute trash," I said.

Freeman aimed a punch. I barely ducked in time. His fist flew into the armrest of the sofa. I let a fist sink into his stomach, making him lose his breath. I was about to light a cigarette when I felt Freeman's open hand slap me across the cheek. The cigarette flew away, landing on my mattress. He looked thin, but he had good speed. Another fist threw me down onto the living room table, which broke in half.

All the old shit bubbled to the surface. We started fighting like madmen, rolling around on the floor and throwing punches as if our lives depended on it. After a while of beating the crap out of each other, we both lay there, exhausted and bloody. I crawled to the mattress and picked up the cigarette. I passed out shortly after.

I woke up the next day, got up, and dusted myself off. I needed to pee as if a thousand beers had come and now wanted to go. The apartment looked like a bomb had gone off. Clothes, beer cans, books, splinters from the table.

Freeman, the damn scoundrel, had locked himself in the bathroom. I heard him snoring in there. I banged on the door.

"Freeman, open the door you old fool, I need to pee," I tried.

He didn't answer. This was the kind of shit that happened when you tried to help someone. It felt like my bladder was going to explode at any moment. I peed in a beer can. I hoped I wouldn't accidentally drink from it later. Shortly after, Freeman came out. He was holding the bathroom rug.

"What are you going to do with the rug?" I said. Freeman looked like someone had asked him to recite the value of pi.

"It's my shirt," Freeman said

"Whatever you say. Charlie's probably on his way now," I said, gesturing towards the clock.

We went out into the yard to meet him. Charlie was a man trying hard to find something to do with his life, but honestly, he hadn't done a thing. He mostly sat at home reading Shakespeare or other pretentious stuff. Or translating poems from English to Swedish. He thought there was something magical about that.

Charlie drove into the yard with his little red Ford. He screeched to a halt, tackled the door open, fell out, got up, and staggered towards us where we stood by the door. He had neck problems and used alcohol as a pain-relieving miracle cure. He stumbled up the stairs, almost breaking his neck again, but instead of getting angry, he laughed heartily. He was one of those who laughed at his own misery, as if life was a circus and he was the main act.

"Hey Hilding!" he shouted, and I saw he had a bottle of whiskey in his hand.

We went into the apartment and Freeman showed us what he wanted us to carry out to the car. Even though Charlie was drunk as a skunk, he started carrying stuff. There was some kind of camaraderie in it all.

"How have you been, Charlie?" I asked.

"Oh, thanks for asking, thanks for asking," said Charlie.

"What are you doing now? Working at all?" I said.

"I saw a guy fucking an exhaust pipe yesterday," said Charlie.

"Oh, where?" I said.

"It was me. It was me fucking an exhaust pipe," said Charlie and nodded towards his car.

We carried out most of the stuff that needed to be taken to Salem and set off.

"Drive carefully now, Charlie, I don't want to be featured on the seven o'clock news," I said.

"There are two kinds of people, those who drive and those who shut the hell up," said Charlie

We arrived at the new place and started unloading the stuff. Grimly, we ran up and down the stairs in silence. Each of us battling our own demons.

BIGFOOT

I was down at the pub with Freeman. It was a small joint, only six tables, and the lighting was nice, not too dark. It was our place, and the guy behind the bar would fix whatever you asked for.

"So, how's work?" Freeman asked.

"All good. You?" I said.

"I have a colleague who seems interested," he said.

"There you go," I said.

"Yeah, she's only 26 though," said Freeman.

"Alright, alright," I said.

I took a sip of beer and let my gaze drift away from the table, out through the window, to the street. Darkness had the city in its grip, the snow fell, and it looked like some kind of miracle was at the door. People hurried by, cars passed, and everything seemed to just happen. I wanted to be out there instead. We stepped out into what had turned from a clear day when we arrived, to a dark evening when we left.

"We should head out into some deep woods," Freeman said.

"Yeah. Hell yeah," I said.

"Pitch a tent to lie in and wait for Bigfoot," Freeman said.

"Maybe we need to go to some really deep woods then, like Oregon or something?" I said.

"They've done detailed studies on that famous Bigfoot film, you know, and concluded that if it was a man in a suit, he'd have to be over 2 meters tall," Freeman said, and continued: "Another thing they analyzed was the proportion between the legs, body, and arms."

"So, what did they conclude?" I asked.

"I don't remember the details, but the proportions and gait also argued against it being a man in a suit," Freeman replied, and continued: "I heard a lecture by a Swedish biologist who claims Bigfoot is an unknown species. Nothing paranormal. All the evidence is there except for a body. He had been to the west coast and spent time with various hunters who had spent their entire lives in the woods, and practically all of them had one or two Bigfoot encounters. Compared to pumas, they also had maybe one or two such encounters."

I believed every word and was ready to head to the west coast with Freeman, just say the word and I'd get on a plane. I wasn't much of a woodsman, and neither was Freeman, so we'd probably die out there, but maybe it would have been worth it.

When I got home that night, I cursed that Ingrid, who I was freeloading at, lived so centrally. I wished that the woods were at my doorstep. Then I would have sat on the porch with a cup of tea, staring out into the woods, alert to any movement. I could almost smell the pine and resin as I sat daydreaming on Ingrid's couch on the third floor, overlooking the city. I could hear twigs and branches snap, a bird suddenly darting away from its perch. Ingrid startled me when she broke the spell. I hadn't noticed she had come into the living room until she spoke to me.

"Did you see the house I sent you?" she asked.

She spent a lot of time online looking for houses, she wanted to get out of the rental she was living in.

"Damn, you scared me, I thought it was Bigfoot for a second," I said.

"What?" said Ingrid.

"Nah, I was just daydreaming," I said.

"Have you seen the house?" she asked again.

"No, was it in the woods?" I wondered.

Ingrid gave up and left.

The beers at the pub had whetted my appetite for more, so I poured myself a glass of whiskey and checked my phone for a party. I fired off a text to half of my contacts, then leaned back and waited.

"We're at a pub," Lydia answered.

I downed the whiskey, grabbed a beer from the fridge, and headed to the pub. Lydia was there with Buckley, Warren, Lily, and a woman I hadn't met before.

"Buckley is explaining what an incel he is," Lydia said.

"But am I wrong?" Buckley said.

"What did I miss?" I asked.

"Well, here's the thing," Buckley said, taking a swig of beer before continuing, "90% of women today carry thinly veiled men-are-pigs' opinions. So, for me, as a man, it's damn nice not to hear that I'm a pig every day, since I'm single and live alone. There's a reason I'm single, you know."

"There's a reason all right," Lydia said. Buckley laughed heartily, but I sensed an anger behind the laughter. His eyes were dark, and his teeth weren't exactly white. He was ready to die for his message. Too bad no one understood what the hell it was.

Time came and went, and so did the drinks. Everything became just a blur. I went to the bathroom, saw in the mirror that I was squinting. I started talking to myself in the mirror.

"Ah, Hilding!" I said, sticking a cigarette in my mouth, "how the fuck are you?"

"Feels like the high is wearing off, first all the right synapses fire in the brain, but then comes the fall, the opponents score three quick goals, BANG, BANG, BANG, and you're left there with your dick in your hand and Satan himself sitting beside you, and you've given the money to the wife, the time to the kids, the lust to the porn, the hope to the booze, all you have left to give is your soul and they want that too, but not today old friend, not today," I said, chuckling and nodding.

"Who are you talking to?" Lily asked outside the door. I started laughing heartily instead of answering. Yeah, who the hell am I talking to? After some more insightful monologues, I strode out of the bathroom.

"Should we go to your place or mine?" I said to Lily.

"Yours?" she said.

"That's not possible," I said, and so we went to her place.

Lily unlocked the door and stepped aside to let me in first. I lost my balance and flew through the door like Superman, only to land like any old drunk.

"Are you okay?" Lily asked.

"That's the problem with you women, you have so much sympathy. Can't you just laugh at me?" I said.

"Please, I can't hear any more about male versus female after all Buckley's rants," Lily said.

"Buckley... There's something entertaining about a 35-year-old guy acting like a 14-year-old girl," I said, chuckling heartily.

"Or a 14-year-old boy, I mean," I added, trying to smooth over any offense.

I scrambled back to my feet and went to the liquor cabinet, fished out a bottle of whiskey, and then headed to the kitchen to grab a glass. As I poured the whiskey, I felt a hand on my shoulder. I glanced down at my blurry shoulder. I thought I saw a hairy ape hand on my shoulder.

"Take it easy with the booze," said a deep male voice behind me. I knew I was alone in the kitchen but nodded anyway. Because I also knew there was an ape in a suit standing behind me. Maybe I had finally lost my mind.

"Who was that woman?" Lily asked, standing in the kitchen doorway. She must've seen I was lost in thought, because she continued, "Are you okay?"

"What are you talking about?" I said, ignoring the fact that I had just hallucinated an ape in a suit.

"There was a woman at our table I'd never seen before, did you talk to her?" Lily said.

"I can't even argue with you, I don't even know what the fuck you're talking about," I said, but then I remembered.

"No, wait, I know who you're talking about," I said, and got a clear picture of her. "I think her name was Chelsea."

I saw her in my mind's eye, beautiful as a painting. Her piercing blue eyes, somehow sad. I fell into a trance.

"Okay, Chelsea," Lily said.

I took out my phone and booked an appointment with a therapist online.

"What are you doing?" Lily asked.

"Changing my relationship status on Facebook," I said.

I put the phone away and noticed the room spinning. My eyelids felt like lead, and I passed out on the couch, but woke up now and then to Lily riding my fairly erect penis.

CRYING ON A MONDAY

He had it all figured out, last chance, all or nothing. He was going to tell her, tell her how he felt. But he was an idiot. She hated people, she hated him. That's why I loved her too, she hated everyone. I can respect that in a person.

We were piling brush in the woods. It was slow, boring, drawn-out, Monday, uncomfortable. He was uninteresting, dumb, ugly, clumsy, indecent. I was tired. Tired from the weekend's many White Russians. I drank and drank but couldn't get drunk. I wanted to find women, but I didn't even see one. It was one of many worthless weekends. Out at the bar, I ran into an old classmate of mine.

"Do you miss junior high, Hilding?" he asked.

"No," I said.

"Would you want to do it over?" he asked.

"No," I said.

"I would want to do it over," he said.

"Do it over and do it right, or what?" I asked.

"No, just like we did it," he said.

He was a lost soul. I looked at him, he was truly lost. I had to get out of here, he was dragging me down. I lit a cigarette inside so I would get thrown out. It didn't take long before the beasts came to get rid of me.

"Perverted ape bastards," I yelled as I reached for my White Russian. My ex had argued, "There's nothing wrong with apes, they're smart." She was a good woman, she meant a lot to me, really, but sometimes you have to put a noun before "bastards". But of course, I agreed with her. The apes shouldn't have to be compared to these swine. Not the swine either.

I downed the drink and forgot about Monday. Monday as it was now, classic Monday. I had cried today, oh yes, how I had cried.

"Do you remember, Hilding, do you remember when we had gym class, but you forgot your sportswear at home?" my old classmate asked.

"I don't even remember your name. Why are you talking to me? Aren't you here to find a woman like sensible people?" I said.

"You went to the store and stole twelve beers, and we shared them in the sauna," he said.

I don't trust people who feel good on Mondays. This guy, my colleague, he felt good. He was as annoying as he was every other day of the week. Never any asocial tendencies. That bothers me, there's something peculiar about a man who never wants to be alone.

He walked around farting, burping, driving too fast, saying girls were whores, stretching, warming up all the time, peeling branches, and whipping the ground and trees. What enormous forces had I upset to even have to meet this person, I wondered, while he rambled on about a bunch of crap.

Now he was going to make his move. Now it was all or nothing. I wished him all the luck, but at the same time, I was worried for her. Did she have the sense to reject him? Did she know what a pig he was? She was a hell of a woman in my book, a real firecracker, I hoped she would understand what she deserved. I could love her until the sun burned out and the world ended if she let me.

A girl had come up to me at the bar:
"Hey Hilding! Do you remember me?" she said.
"Hey! Of course I do!" I lied.
"I have a boyfriend now," she said.
He joined us and immediately started telling me he had lived in this and that country, and other fancy things I immediately forgot. He got jealous of me right away, I got the feeling he hit her. I just tried to get away. Why did she even talk to me?

"Well, you have a good one then," I said, and now, now it was Monday, and another colleague with a long scraggly beard came up to me and said:

"I want to take mushrooms, do you want to join?" and all these damn animals swarmed around me, saw me as one of them, and I hated them all, and yes, it was Monday, and yes, I had cried, many tears, but there were still more to come.

THE MAN BEHIND THE DOOR

"Where's the old ball-and-chain?" Charlie asked.

"Or did you become a faggot and break up with her?" he continued, licking his lips.

I studied his disgusting face. He was gay, I knew it, but he refused to admit it.

"Why are you licking your lips?" I asked, glaring at him.

"What? I had crumbs in my mustache," Charlie said.

"The missus couldn't come today," Frey began. "I told her she had to stay home and clean today," he continued, chuckling heartily.

I suspected Frey was lying, he would never dare to say something like that, but I had been wrong before, so I said nothing. Instead, I poked at my slice of cake with the dessert fork but changed my mind and took a sip of coffee instead. It tasted bitter and cold. I took another sip. And another.

"Damn, you're really guzzling that down," Frey said.

I drained the rest of the coffee cup and went to get a refill. My whole body was shaking. I held my hand above the table to show how much I was trembling.

"Damn," Charlie said.

"I'm so damn tired, the coffee doesn't seem to work. I need stronger stuff," I said. My eyes ached and I had dark circles under them.

"Why are you so tired?" Frey wondered.

I remembered the night. I was lying in bed, trying to sleep when there was a knock on the door. I got up and went to peek through the peephole. I saw nothing, someone was covering it.

"Who's there?" I called out.

No answer. Luckily, I had a security chain on the door, so I opened it. I heard someone moving back with the door. Through the crack, I could only see the hallway. I tried again:

"Who's there?"

No answer that time either. What the hell do I do now, I thought.

"I'm closing the door," I said, hopeful for a reaction.

Slowly, I closed the door, but there were no protests from the hallway. I locked it and looked through the peephole again. Whoever was on the other side was still covering it, so I saw nothing. Perplexed, I stood by the door and watched. I couldn't just go back to bed with some lunatic standing there covering the peephole. I went to the kitchen and got a beer from the fridge. I popped it open and took a few sips, then went back to the front door. The peephole was still black.

"I can stand here all night," I said, taking another sip of beer.

"I've got beer here," I continued, immediately puzzled as to why I had said that.

Maybe it was to signal that I had settled in by the peephole. Either way, it didn't get a reaction. I went to the living room and grabbed my Bluetooth speaker, then returned to the peephole. I played some music to the old bastard.

I heard the echo of a foot tapping to the beat in the hallway. The beer was going down easy, so I went to the fridge and grabbed two more, then went back. I put one on the hat shelf for later, and opened the other, took a sip, then returned to the peephole.

"Sooner or later, you'll have to move your hand," I said.

I got an idea. I took the beer from the hat shelf and opened the door again, with the security chain on. Through the crack, I slid the beer along the floor, then closed the door and returned to the peephole. At first, nothing. Then, someone bent down, took the beer, and quickly put their hand back over the peephole. It looked like a man. He was wearing a black jacket, that's all I saw.

Time passed, and I started getting drunk. I got the hiccups and tried to swallow them away, but it was useless. I was in the middle of googling how to get rid of hiccups when I heard the door of the neighbor across the hall open.

"Hello," I heard my neighbor, Mrs. Andersson, say from the hallway.

"Hello," my tormentor replied.

It was a man, now that was confirmed at least.

"Mrs. Andersson," I called out, "who's covering my peephole?"

She didn't hear me, or she didn't want to get involved, but I got no response. The chance to find out my tormentor's identity had slipped through my fingers, and it made me upset.

"You goddamn cocksucker, why are you terrorizing regular folks? I have to get up early tomorrow, let me sleep for fuck's sake," I said.

I heard him snort.

"What do you have to get up early for, you loafer?" he replied.

I was boiling. How dare he question whether I had to get up early or not. He doesn't know what I have to do. I recalled a wise man's words; if someone calls you a dog, look back and see if you have a tail. If you don't, what's the problem? With that, I tried to calm down and return to the present moment.

"I know what you want, I've read about people like you," I said.

"Oh really, I had my doubts that you could even read," he replied.

He really knew how to push my buttons. I crumpled the beer can I was holding and cursed to myself. I looked around, several crumpled beer cans were scattered around me. I felt the tears welling up in my eyes, and finally, I broke down. I started sobbing but tried to do it quietly.

"Are you crying?" I heard from the hallway.

I didn't answer. Instead, I curled up in the fetal position and let the tears flow. I don't know how long I lay there before I fell asleep, but when the morning dawned, I was still on the floor by the front door. I got up and took a deep breath. Then I peeked through the peephole. All I saw was the hallway and Mrs. Andersson's door. I sighed with relief.

This came to mind as I sat in the café with Frey and Charlie.

"Why are you so tired?" they asked.

"It's a long story," I said.

A man placed his hands on our table. He leaned down and looked at me.

"A long story, you say?" he said.

I immediately recognized his voice. It was him, my tormentor. A middle-aged man with a weathered face. He'd seen a thing or two in his days. I got scared.

"S-sorry for calling you a cocksucker," I said.

He fixed his eyes on me and grabbed me by the neck. He pressed my face into the cake on my plate.

"Don't do it again," he said.

"Sorry, sorry," I said.

Frey and Charlie sat wide-eyed, watching. I waited for them to intervene, but they were completely paralyzed. He let go, and I sat back up. I reached for a napkin, but he yanked it from my hand and ate it. Then he grabbed my coffee cup and downed the rest.

"Have you even considered that maybe I'm also tired?" he said.

He took my dessert fork and scooped up a big chunk of the mashed cake.

"S-sorry," I said.

"Well, selfish idiots are a dime a dozen, I'm used to it," he said, shoving the cake into his mouth, before turning on his heel.

We watched as he strode out of the café, paused, held out a hand to check if it was raining, saw that it was, pulled up his hood, and walked away with his hands in his pockets. We saw him meet Frey's wife, greet her, then continue into a mall. We still sat in silence as Frey's wife walked in.

"I've cleaned the whole damn house, Frey," she said.

DISCIPLINE

She had big tits. I had nothing. She had curves in all the right places. I had a penis. On a good day I could get it up.

"I'm heading to India for three months," she said.

I looked up from staring at her chest.

"That's great, but according to the news, it's the most dangerous country for women right now," I said.

She started to smile and stared at me for a moment.

"Are you worried about me?" she asked.

"I know you can take care of yourself," I said. "But stuff like that can leave its mark."

"Stuff like what?" she wondered.

"I don't know, a bottle up your ass," I said

She got all indignant and stood up. I thought she was going to leave, but she just went to the bathroom. I started imagining what she was doing in there. Did she unbutton her jeans and pull them down to her ankles? And then put her thumbs inside each side of the panties, and pulled them down to her thighs? Maybe she then sat down on the toilet ring and let a hot jet of piss whip the inside of the toilet. Maybe she could piss on me one day. She came back to the table. While still standing she gulped down the last of her coffee.

"I have to go," she said, wrapping her scarf around her neck.

"Take care," I said and got up for a hug.

"It was nice to see you, it's been so long," she said.

"You never visited me in the joint," I said.

"I thought you were a murderer," she said.

"Still…," I replied.

"Come to me tonight for a proper goodbye," she said, stroking my dick.

When Johnny died, no one offered their condolences. When Johnny died, it was cold, gray, and dark. When Johnny died, I was drunk enough for four grown men.

"Johnny, you damn pig," I said.

He didn't answer, because he was dead. When Johnny died, I was young, it was a long time ago. I'm old now, but I'm still alive. I outlived them all, the whole gang. Johnny, Jason, Bobby, Nicole, Tony.

I'd do anything for a fix. When Johnny died, I did anything. I'd do anything for a fix. When Johnny died, I was in prison for five years. I met David in the joint. When David died, I did anything for a fix.

Destruction is my legacy. I haven't cried since I was a kid. They can't get to me anymore. Come on, do your worst. I haven't cried since 1994.

I was there when Jason died. I stuck the knife in his throat. I did anything. No one cares, as long as the stuff is cheap. When Jason died, I saw Satan in a window. He looked at me, he laughed at me. I threw the knife at the window. I did anything.

But it turns out it wasn't me who did it. My mind played tricks on me back then, false memories. I'm a free man nu, I'm clean now, like a virgin. Like a white lamb. It's easy to get stained when you're so clean.

I went home and painted my face black and red, my dick too. I had bought some booze at the store and condoms at Walmart. I slipped a condom on my dick, then set off.

"Goodbye, friends," I shouted to the fish.

"Goodbye," they didn't reply.

I drank from the booze like a madman. I took the commuter train to the southern station. I was heading to her place. It was a battlefield, a holy crusade, I was so damn lonely.

I pulled out my dick in the stairwell. The booze was hitting hard, I began doubting that I would make it. I got down on all fours, crawling. One step at a time. She lived on the fourth floor. Typical of my luck, I thought. I took a swig, two, three swigs of booze. I was drunk, I was sick in the head. My dick dragged against the steps, leaving a black and red streak all the way up to the fourth floor. The condom fell off somewhere on the way. It was a war, and you had to expect casualties. I've lost many battles, but I haven't lost the war, not yet, I thought.

I lay down. My legs were on the stairs, my upper body on the fourth-floor landing. My dick rested just above the last step. My face was black and red, staining the floor. I took another swig, awaiting death. It's happening, I said. This is it.

I took out the condom pack, held it in front of my face, looked at it. I smiled and gripped it tightly. I let my hand fall to the side, still clutching the pack. I pulled out the booze from my inner pocket, poured some on my dick, then down my throat. I laughed out loud. I'm going to be something, I thought, I'm going to show those bastards, all of them. I laughed. What a damn genius I am, that I hadn't thought of this before. It's all about discipline, I thought. Like Forsberg or Gretzky. Success doesn't come to the lazy. It takes hard damn work and iron discipline. That's what it's all about.

CONFESSIONS OF A COCK BEARER

Ingrid came into my room.

"You've got a call," she said.

"Who is it?" I said.

"It's John, he wants to give you some movie recommendations," she said.

John, a former cock bearer, former human. He had problems with his dick. Couldn't get it up. Didn't matter which woman was in front of him, he'd fail every time.

"Take it easy, kid, you're not the first or the last with that old problem," I said.

He was in love with the cashier at the kiosk. She stood there serving hot dogs all day long. Sloppy hotdogs, like John's dick. He used to go down there and buy hot dogs like hell. He'd hear the old guys talk about her, the love of his life.

"Have you seen the ugly one at the kiosk?" they'd say.

He'd clench his fist in his coat pocket. Sometimes he'd go outside, bawling his eyes out. If only he could get it up, he'd give her everything. Now he didn't even dare to approach her.

She wasn't much to look at, I agreed with the old guys. But on the other hand, I've been with worse.

The woman who had chosen me on the other hand was a delight to look at. But she had a husband, she felt stuck. She would never leave him, of course.

"What should I do, Hilding? I want to be with you," she could say to me.

I didn't want her to leave her husband for me, that would put such pressure on me.

"Just vibe with the universe, baby," I said then.

"How do you do that?" she asked.

"Be passive, do nothing," I said.

Back to John. I was done with John. He had compromised me for the last time at Johnny's funeral. After the ceremony, John, Freeman, and I stood outside the church.

"I'll show you some pictures of Johnny," John had said.

"It's fine," Freeman replied.

John pulled out his phone and started showing pictures of Johnny, and himself.

"This one's good, Johnny and I were fishing," John said.

Suddenly, nude pictures popped up on his phone screen.

"This is an ex of mine. She was wild," John said.

He kept showing pictures of her, sure, she was hot, but it was inappropriate. By the time we noticed, Johnny's aunt had gotten a little too close.

"What are you boys doing?" she asked.

She reached over my shoulder to see the phone screen.

I took the phone from my mom.

"John! What the hell kind of letter combinations are you suffering from?"

"I have to tell you what happened to my buddy. He had a thing for his girlfriend's friend. So, this friend was over visiting one time, and my buddy, well, he got turned on, of course. He excused himself to go to the bathroom. He pulled up some pictures of her on her Instagram and got going, you know. But the idiot accidentally liked an old damn picture of her on the beach in a bikini or something. So, his girlfriend and the friend were chatting in the kitchen when her phone vibrates with a notification, and it's this damn fool liking an old half naked Instagram picture of her," John said.

"The 'friend' is you, isn't it?" I said.

"So, anyway, I saw on Facebook that you wanted movie tips," John said.

"Yeah? So, comment on my Facebook status? Why the hell do you always call?"

"I liked The Sixth Sense with Bruce Willis."

A REAL MAN

The internet had been down all day, and Buckley was stuck with the same old crap on TV. When Buckley heard his neighbor out in the stairwell, it felt natural for him to rush to the peephole. Maybe she had something sexy on? A tank top? Tight pants? Buckley needed something to jerk off to, and he needed it now.

She had puffy sweatpants and a hoodie, but it had to do. He pulled out his dick, she pulled out her keys. She inserted the key into the lock, slowly, in and out, in and out. Buckley moaned a little too loudly, she turned towards his door. Her mouth looked nice, great shape. Buckley was about to come, any second now. But she opened the door and went inside, he didn't make it in time. Feeling defeated, he went to the kitchen. He had potatoes on the stove, the water had been boiling for an hour, but the potatoes were still raw. Damn potatoes, he thought. He cut them in half, he didn't care if nutrients boiled away, he wasn't going to wait two hours for some damn potatoes.

When the potatoes were finally done, he put them on a plate and started eating. But he had forgotten to fry the steaks to go with them, it took so damn long to boil the potatoes that he forgot about it. So, it was just potatoes for dinner.

Buckley started wondering what the neighbor was up to, maybe I should ring her doorbell? She was quite good-looking, a few years younger, maybe she was feeling it too. Who doesn't like to fuck? God, I'm so lonely, Buckley thought. He had been alone since he was a little kid.

Buckley thought about his dad. He died when Buckley was six. They were out walking, Dad carrying Buckley on his shoulders, when they saw a burglary. Dad, the hero he was, ran over to stop it. The burglar shot him in the head. Buckley sat by the body when the guy who shot his dad came up to Buckley.

"I'm sorry, kid, I had to," he said, then took off.

Buckley met him a few years later. His dad, I mean. Turns out Dad faked the whole thing.

"I wanted out of the mess," his dad said, "away from you and your mother."

Apparently, Dad knew the "burglar", and it was all a ruse. The cops didn't have much to go on, just a six-year-old's word, but they never found a body, of course. Maybe Mom knew too, now that Buckley thought about it, but she never said anything.

Buckley had told everyone at school that his dad got shot, but when it came out that he was alive, Buckley got bullied. They used to beat him up good during recess.

"You're a liar!" they screamed.

Buckley's nostalgia trip was interrupted by sounds from the stairwell. Time to finish the job, he thought, and ran to the peephole. It wasn't her, it was another neighbor, a guy.

Goddamnit, Buckley thought, but it will have to do. He pulled out the old dick again.

Buckley wasn't always like this. He had a wife once. He used to lie in the bed they shared for all those years, lost in memories of her, of her amazing body. He used to close his eyes and go at it, thinking of her, but it didn't work. It never did. He'd look up at the bedroom door, waiting for her, as if she'd come around the corner any moment now. If she just finished whatever she was doing, she'd come back to Buckley. But she wouldn't come, never again. It was three years ago he found her. Her lifeless body hanging from a rope around her neck. Buckley had just finished work down at the factory. He made steel there, Buckley and the other guys. That was his life back then, the plant and the wife. They went hand in hand, because when Buckley lost his wife, he lost the plant. He just couldn't handle it at the time.

Buckley went to the kitchen, had a bit of whiskey, just a glass or two. Buckley didn't cry, Dad said tears were for faggots and women, and damn if that wasn't true. A real man doesn't cry.

EMPTY LOVE

I was on some flight, heading somewhere. An angel sat in the same row as me. She was by the window, and I was by the aisle. An old lady sat between us. She was old. Too old, and she knew it. She went to the bathroom. There was just an empty seat between me, a former human, and Miss Universe, eternal happiness. I loved her, and she loved me. I said nothing, neither did she. It wouldn't have worked between us; I focused on my career, she wanted someone else, someone serious. So did I.

The guy in front of me reclined his seat for some damn reason. Leaned back. I wanted to punch him in the face. But it was hopeless, of course, I had already lost. He was my superior, but I gave him a fight. They all mocked me. Everyone on that damn plane. But I had hidden talents, I knew it. She was Eve, and I was just me, not Adam. I wanted to be, but I never was.

I had been drinking wine for three days with Freeman and Frey. They could really drink wine. The wine hated me, I always got too drunk. Today I just want to get it over with, find some idiot with a gun and get shot, end the suffering for us all. Yesterday, I loved life.

She was a goddess, but she doesn't like me that way. She doesn't like me at all, she hates me. I need her, she makes me whole. But she probably has a man. Some dude with a paycheck, beard, and glasses. She could really crush my heart. It was hers to treat as she wished.

Anyway, it doesn't matter. Now it's about survival. Surviving this damn day. That's where I need to focus. And piecing together the days that have passed, what the hell happened. I had no memories, it might as well have been a dream, all of it. Reality came back too fast and too rough. I should try to talk to her. But it probably won't go well. To have common interests, you first need to have interests, and I don't.

"Have I told you about Frey?" I said.

"Do I know you," she said.

So, I told her about Frey.

Play 'Get Happy'," he used to say. I wasn't sure about the chords, but I didn't dare say no to him. I sat at the piano, started playing, and he began to sing.

"Forget your troubles, come on get happy, you better chase all your cares away."

He stopped and looked at me. I had played the wrong chord, and he heard it. My ear rang, my cheek stung. A solid slap sent me to the floor. I crawled up from the ground, got to my feet. I felt his fist sink into my stomach. I went down again, gasping for air, praying to God, Ra, Shiva, anyone.

He slept on the floor, right on the floor, no pillow, just a thin blanket over him. He set the alarm for 4:30 AM, and when it rang, he jumped up and shadowboxed, then down again, push-ups, sit-ups, chin-ups, squats, out into the cold to jog in a t-shirt, the whole damn routine. When he came home, he took a cold shower.

He used to kick me in the stomach at 6 AM.

"Time to wake up you little cocksucker. Give me 10."

I dropped to the floor, started doing push-ups. 1, 2, 3, 4… A hard kick to the stomach sent me to the floor. I looked up, he was shadowboxing.

"Footwork," he said, "remember, footwork is important."

"How come you were living with Frey?" she asked.

"It was either that or the park bench," I said.

"The park bench almost sounds better," she said.

"It's not, trust me," I said.

We kissed, we got together, we got married, and then we were happy for the rest of our days. We had five kids, three cars, a two-story villa, I got a job as a manager at an IT firm, and she became a well-respected player in the real estate business. I've kept my hair neatly combed and my suit pressed every day—and I haven't had a drop to drink—since that flight 15 years ago. If you're reading this baby, I just want you to know that I love you.

FINNEGAN'S FINAL WARNING

"Fucking bastards. What the hell is your problem? You're ten fucking people, I'm alone, cocksuckers. I have worked all my life, I have no money. Fucking pussies. You fucking name it. Shut the fuck up."

Mr. Thomas was pissed off. He'd been drinking for three days straight. He just wanted to go into the store and grab something, but a group of immigrants pushed him over the edge. His IQ wasn't particularly high, but he had a lot of faith in himself. He rarely questioned his opinions or life decisions. Finnegan told him there are smarter people he should listen to instead.

The immigrants sat outside the grocery store in the blazing sun. They said nothing, just watched him. Finnegan had just gotten out of the car when he saw the spectacle. Mr. Thomas walked away, then turned back and fired off another rant, then made another attempt to get to the bus stop, only to stop and turn back again.

"Mr. Thomas," Finnegan said, "have you gone mad?"

Finnegan was his psychologist. Mr. Thomas had been seeing Finnegan for six months.

"Thank God you're here, I fear for my life," Mr. Thomas said.

"Please, Mr. Thomas, you're harassing these poor people," Finnegan said.

Finnegan opened the passenger door of gis old Ford and gestured for Mr. Thomas to get in. Mr. Thomas sat down, and Finnegan closed the door. Finnegan looked at the immigrants, they seemed shocked.

"I apologize for Mr. Thomas," Finnegan said as he jumped into the driver's seat.

Finnegan started the car and rolled out of the parking lot. He smacked the glove compartment, which only opened that way, and fished out a half-full bottle of brandy, taking a good swig straight from the bottle.

"Would you like some brandy, Mr. Thomas?" Finnegan asked.

Mr. Thomas greedily grabbed the bottle and took a few hefty gulps.

"You missed our last appointment," Finnegan said, snatching the bottle from his hand.

"It's been a lot lately. My mother passed away," Mr. Thomas said.

"Don't lie to me, Mr. Thomas. Your mother passed away when you were a child," Finnegan said.

Finnegan brought the brandy bottle to my mouth. Mr. Thomas had tainted the entire neck of the bottle with his cigarette-smoke-laden breath.

"You've had half the bottle in your mouth, Mr. Thomas," Finnegan said. "You have sucked off the bottle, like a prostitute. Do you ever fantasize about pleasing men's penises Mr. Thomas?"

Mr. Thomas immediately burst out,

"What the hell are you saying? Don't come at me with such accusations."

"As your psychologist, this is very important for me to know," Finnegan said, holding up the bottle in front of Mr. Thomas.

"I heard of a man whose wife used to rape him with a bottle much like this one. It was his neighbor who told me," Finnegan said.

Mr. Thomas tried to snatch the bottle, but Finnegan pulled it away.

"He's a confidant of mine. He sleeps with a gun under his pillow," Finnegan said.

Finnegan handed Mr. Thomas the brandy, which he greedily gulped down.

"Why does he see a psychologist, you ask? Various reasons, including that his father abused him when he was a little boy. Once, when they were out in the woodshed..." Finnegan started, when Mr. Thomas interrupted him.

"Let me out here...," he said.

Finnegan smacked the steering wheel with both hands.

"Mr. Thomas!" he shouted. "Don't you know to be quiet when someone is talking to you?"

Finnegan straightened the tie hanging outside my shirt. No jacket needed on warm days like these.

"Anyway, where was I? Yes, they were out in the woodshed, as I said before you so rudely interrupted me. His father had told him about the time he killed a man. Have you ever killed someone, Mr. Thomas?" Finnegan asked.

Finnegan noticed Mr. Thomas sitting with his mouth open, looking like an idiot. Mr. Thomas didn't answer. He seemed close to drooling, which made him suck in his saliva and close his mouth.

"You must understand, Mr. Thomas, that as a psychologist, I know better than most. I know what murder can do to a person. You could never understand that Mr. Thomas, you're not well-read enough. You lack the brain capacity to even become well-read," Finnegan said.

Mr. Thomas reminded Finnegan of a dog. He listened, but the words meant nothing to him. He wasn't intelligent enough to understand, and even if he was, his vocabulary didn't contain enough words to grasp or engage in a deeper conversation.

"That's why you belong to society's absolute bottom tier, Mr. Thomas. And that's also why I belong to the elite. The same elite that keeps society functioning," Finnegan said.

Mr. Thomas had finished the brandy, so Finnegan smacked the glove compartment open again. This time he fished out an unopened bottle of vodka. He cracked it open and took a few solid gulps before handing it to Mr. Thomas. Finnegan glanced at him as he brought the bottle to his lips. Mr. Thomas reminded Finnegan of filth. A grease stain on a white shirt, refusing to disappear no matter how many times you wash it.

Finnegan pulled the car over to the side of the road. He left the engine running but got out and walked around the car, yanked open the passenger door, and grabbed Mr. Thomas firmly. Finnegan dragged him out, and he landed on the ground, looking thoroughly surprised. Finnegan snatched the vodka, slipping it into his pocket. Then Finnegan grabbed Mr. Thomas's jacket and threw him into the ditch. Mr. Thomas rolled right down into the water, making it impossible for Finnegan not to smile.

"Never miss an appointment again," Finnegan said, "You see, Mr. Thomas, and this is something you obviously can't relate to, but my time is incredibly valuable. You dedicate your time to decadence, that's no secret. But know this, Mr. Thomas: you don't waste the elite's time without consequences."

Finnegan raised his arm to check the time. 12:34 it read.

"Now it's time for me to go, Mr. Thomas. I have an appointment with a confidant in just 30 minutes," Finnegan said.

Finnegan jumped in the car and sped off. He fished the bottle from his pocket, took a few good gulps, then tossed it out the window. He drove up a mountain, then veered onto a field. He floored it and plowed through the field, and then onwards, up a cliff and over its edge.

THE VENETIAN SHADOW

I was living with Freeman in a one-room apartment. He was a former Buddhist, former teetotaler, former exercise enthusiast, now an alcoholic and aspiring writer. He had nothing going for him, the poor bastard. He also had an unreasonable circadian rhythm, I never managed to adapt.

I opened a beer, downed the bastard. I was starving, thirsty, it had been a long time. Some crap from the grocery store, the cheapest brand.

I asked Freeman what the hell kind of plans he had made for himself for the day. He was going on a date, and he invited me to join him. It felt strange, pathetic even, but I had nothing else going on. I hadn't changed my underwear or put on deodorant for four days.

We were going to a bar. Freeman walked next to the date, Alice, and they talked about all sorts of things, laughed, and had fun. I walked behind them, like some appendage. But I did a good job once I got into it. I had a brandy in my inner pocket that I sipped on now and then. I injected witty remarks and brilliant observations. Both Freeman and Alice appreciated my observations and laughed heartily. Eventually, I was the only one laughing. I started to slur, I was living it up. I felt like a dog.

We stopped by a pizzeria, ordered a pizza each, and sat down at a table.

"Have I told you about my friend who was a poker millionaire?" I said.

"No," said Freeman.

"He used to go out to a nightclub and rent a private booth and order champagne," I said.

"That's cool," said Alice.

"Yeah, he once pulled out his dick and pissed under the table," I said.

"Oh, gross...," said Alice.

"Then a girl he liked came over. She stood there at the table chatting with him, all while he was still pissing under the table. She even had it under her shoes. So, when she went to leave, she discovered she was standing in a puddle," I said.

"Oh my god, for real?" said Alice.

"Yes, it's true, I was there, it was crazy. She got so damn mad; she hasn't even talked to ME since then. He really lived the high life back then," I said.

"I don't know how you define 'the high life'...," Alice said.

"He lost everything; he gambled it all away after a night of heavy drinking. He had to move back in with his dad and start work for him as rent... Tragic," I said.

"That sounds awful. Can you see yourself in his situation?" wondered Alice.

"Yeah, it was in fact me," I said.

"Is that so?" Alice said.
"Nah...," I said.

We set off once again towards the bar.
"Let me tell you about this old town," Freeman said.
"This is a building, old as hell. It has some cultural value, but I can't remember what," he continued, pointing at some building.

Freeman's breath smelled of cheap alcohol and bad life decisions. He pulled out a whiskey from his pocket and drank wholeheartedly. Then he started ranting about his life as a Buddhist, teetotaler, librarian, writer, alcoholic, but his heart wasn't really in it. Still, he was starting to get on my nerves.

"You're drinking like a damn animal," I said.
"I like you guys, you're funny," Alice said.

At the bar Alice went to the bathroom for the tenth time. That woman had a small bladder. Or she had something in her inner pocket too.

"Damn it, what have I gotten myself into?" said Freeman, fishing the bottle of whiskey from his pocket. That whiskey was his damn lifesaver.

"I think you're doing a wonderful job," I said.

I looked at my clock. The last train was leaving in eight minutes, so I ran off. I got so caught up in the moment that I forgot to say goodbye.

At the station Freeman caught up with me. I saw him approaching me at the platform, out of breath.

"What the hell are you doing?" he asked.
"What?" I said.
"Why did you just run off like that?" said Freeman.
"I'm just done. I hate this city," I said.

"It was like in a movie. You were like the Venetian Shadow," he said.

"What did Alice say when you just left?" I asked.

"I just said I had to follow you, that you wouldn't find your way home otherwise, that you're kind of retarded. She looked pissed."

The train arrived, and we got on. I drew Freeman in a little notebook I used to carry around. Freeman looked like a washed-up old drunk in the finished picture, and maybe he was just that.

STRAIGHT LIES

We were sitting at the local café, like we always did, especially on rainy Sundays like this one.

"I dreamt I was dating a guy," Charlie said.

I looked down into my coffee cup, stirring it with the spoon, trying to stir as fast as I could without spilling.

"We had been dating for several months in the dream. Me and that guy were at some charity event together, talking to Riley, who was a security guard in the dream. He stood there smiling, not in an obviously mocking way, but still as if he thought I was beneath him now that I had become gay," Charlie continued.

I lifted my gaze from the coffee cup, focused on the window behind Charlie, then further out to the rain-darkened street outside. I saw a woman walk past the window, she was probably close to 40, but she looked good, fresh for her age, or maybe I was just getting old.

"I told Riley I was gay now, and I was fine with it. We fucked each other's asses too, I fucked him and then he fucked me, and you know what the weird part was?" Charlie said.

I brought the cup to my mouth and sipped some coffee, but I had to spit it out right away, it had already gone cold. Instead, I took a bite of the chocolate ball I had bought, the first time in my life I had ever bought one. I reflected on that, why did I buy it now, on this particular day? Was there any explanation for it at all?

"The weird part was that I liked it," Charlie continued.

I fished a cigarette out of the pack and brought it to my mouth, but stopped just before it touched my lips, and looked up at Charlie.

"So, you're gay? Is that what you're trying to say?" I said.

"Nah," Charlie said.

A moment passed and we said nothing. I looked at Charlie, who was sipping his coffee. The way he pursed his lips reminded me of a guy who liked to suck cock. He looked down at my chocolate ball, then at me.

"Can I have a bite?" Charlie said.

"No, I took a dump on it, you little cocksucker," I said.

"Alright then, sorry," said Charlie.

"No, no, forgive *me*," I replied.

We finished our coffee and stepped out into the fresh spring air. It was warm enough to leave the scarf at home, but you could still see your breath. I lit a cigarette when Charlie turned to me.

"What do you have against gays anyway?" Charlie asked.

"Nothing, what do you mean?" I said.

"You always ask if I'm gay," Charlie said.

"I have nothing against gays, I'd consider it myself if it weren't for the fact that I find women very sexy," I said.

Just then, a girl with curves in all the right places walked past us.

"Just look," I said, nodding towards the girl.

"Yeah, you're right," Charlie said.

"Of course I am, I'm always right," I said, putting my arm around him to give him a good shake.

"I'm heading into town," I said.

"Okay, I'll catch up later, I just need to buy something sweet," Charlie said, gesturing towards the kiosk next to the café.

I walked into the main street of the city center and peeked into the many shop windows lined up along the street. Charlie had finished his shopping and spotted me. He snuck up behind me and started tickling me. I quickly turned around and started tickling him back. He parried and got in a few good tickles on me, but I didn't give up. I slipped my hands inside his jacket and shirt and went straight for the skin. He started laughing uncontrollably and we lost our balance and fell to the ground. We rolled around on the main street, tickling each other. After a bit of rolling, we stopped, and he ended up on top of me. He straddled me, sitting there smiling at me like a real sissy. I saw the outline of his hard penis against his jeans.

"I knew it, you're a faggot!" I said, pointing to his erect penis.

"No, it's my phone," Charlie said.

"You're smiling like someone in love," I said, pushing him away.

I got up, feeling violated and angry.

"I'm not gay, for God's sake," Charlie said.

I left Charlie without saying another word. I felt too upset to talk to him any further. I headed home, the clock nearing dinnertime, and I was fed up with people.

I made myself a cup of tea and settled in front of the TV. I was flipping through channels when the phone rang for the fourth time. It was Charlie again. He'll never give up unless I answer and tell him off, I thought, grabbing the phone.

"Hey Hilding, sorry about earlier," he said.

"Stop calling me and stop saying sorry, for fuck's sake, it's annoying," I said.

"Yeah, sorry... But hey, I've got some beers here, why don't I come over and we bury the hatchet?" he suggested.

"Damn it, Charlie. Okay, but no cheap beer," I said.

We ended the call, and I turned my attention back to the TV. I couldn't be bothered to flip through channels anymore, so I left it on the Antiques Roadshow. About ten minutes later, the doorbell rang. I went to open it, and there was Charlie.

"Hey!" he said cheerfully, as if everything was forgiven.

"Hey," I said, but without smiling.

Charlie went to the fridge, pulled out two beers from the bag, and put the rest inside. Then he came to me in the living room and handed me one of the beers.

"What crap are you watching?" Charlie teased.

"What crap? It's the Antiques Roadshow," I said.

Charlie nudged me lightly in the side. I looked at him, he was sitting there smiling.

"You're such an old man," he said.

I nudged him back. He nudged me harder, and I grabbed a pillow and hit him with it. He grabbed his own pillow and hit back. We jumped up on the couch, laughing, and started wrestling standing up. I got him down on the floor and straddled him. I felt something pressing against my ass, and I feared the worst. I slid down along his leg, and sure enough, his erect penis was making his jeans bulge again.

"It's the phone," he said.

"That's not a phone," I said.

"Yes, I swear," he said.

I felt the bulge to check if it was a phone.

"That's not a phone you gay bastard!" I said.

"It is too!" Charlie said.

I unbuttoned his fly and pulled his hard cock out of his underpants. I grabbed it firmly and looked at him accusingly. He looked ashamed.

"Admit it now, you filthy little faggot," I said.

"Ah, what the hell, it has nothing to do with you, I was thinking about Josie," he explained.

He slapped me across the cheek with an open hand, and I flew to the floor. I quickly got back on my feet and gave him a good fist in his stomach. He staggered back but quickly regained his balance and gave me a right hook over my eye. I flew to the floor again, face down. My eye ached, and the room started to spin. He sat over me and pulled down my pants and underpants. I felt something warm and pulsating trying to penetrate my anus. I turned my head back and saw his dick trying to do its thing.

"Okay, okay, you're not gay," I tried to get him to stop.

"Watch yourself, next time you accuse me of something like that, you're in for it," Charlie said, releasing me from his grip.

I kicked Charlie out and sat back down on the couch. A vase was appraised at a million on the Antiques Roadshow, and I wondered why I couldn't have such luck to have a million-dollar vase sitting at home.

THE HALIBUT DILEMMA

It was one of those nights that wanted to kick me in the face and laugh at me when I walked along a forest path in a nature reserve. I saw a girl approaching from the opposite direction. She was wearing dark clothes, a hood over her head. I avoided looking at her, fixing my eyes on the ground, like some timid ape.

"Hi," she said when we got closer to each other.

"Hi," I blurted out at the last second.

I looked up at her and met her gaze, she looked disgusted. She despised my ape demeanor. I began to fear that I had finally gone mad, that she didn't really exist. Even my own chimeras didn't want anything to do with me.

I saw something lying on the ground. I picked up what turned out to be a wallet. I opened it and produced an ID. Shayla Harris. I turned around, but she was long gone. I looked her up on my phone and found her address.

She lived two stairs up. I went up the stairs and stood outside the door. I raised one hand to ring the doorbell but stopped myself. Why should I ring anyway? I won't disturb her. I'll just put it in the mail slot, that's just as well, right? But I long for some kind of social interaction, if only a thank you.

I lowered my hand from the doorbell and took the wallet out of my jacket pocket. I slid it through the mail slot and heard it hit the floor. I turned to leave, when the door was flung open. Terrified, I turned around, expecting Bob, fat, ugly, drunk, angry, and dangerous. But instead, it was her standing in the doorway.

"What took you so long?" she said.

I didn't know what to say, apes don't have coherent thoughts. I managed a "what?".

She turned around and went inside. She was wearing a black tank top and pink panties. She was slim, brunette, pretty, nice ass. I cleared my throat.

"Yeah, well, you happened to drop this,' I said, pointing to the wallet still on the floor.

She had sat down on her couch with her feet on the edge of the table in front. The TV lit her up, shifting colors from white to blue to black. She threw her head back and said:

"You dork, are you coming in or what?"

"Coming in? Yeah, I guess I can do that," I said.

Stiff as a board and terrified, I took off my outer clothes and stood by the TV. My arms and hands hung straight down along my body. My eyes were wide open, terrified.

"So, what size is your TV?" I asked.

"We've met before,' she said.

"Really?" I said.

"You don't remember?' she said.

"Not really, sorry," I said.

She gave me a beer and one thing led to another as is tradition. I started unbuttoning, looking at her as if to get confirmation that I was doing it right. She nodded sarcastically at me.

"Fuck me you beast," she said. Freeman will never believe me, I thought.

I'm not exactly a beast. I'm mostly slim but look kind of fat when I sit down.

Shayla drank like a wild animal. She used to take my bank card to buy booze and cigarettes. Socializing was good for me. We drank and fucked quite a lot, I was hungover almost every day. Shayla worked the fish counter at the grocery store. One day, she brought home a halibut and said, "You want to break up with me."
"Well, I don't know," I replied.
"Yes, you do," Shayla said.
"Okay, baby, whatever you want, but what the hell are you going to do with that halibut?" I said.

She was looking to cook up that big old halibut for some other man. Don't I know it.

MOOSE MEATBALLS

Frey was in town. The atmosphere changed as he moved through the streets, as if the very air vibrated with his presence. We had a few nights ahead of us that would make our livers cry for mercy and salvation.

Freeman was already in good shape early on. He had downed whisky, wine, vodka, and rum at home. A whole orchestra of alcohol played in his bloodstream, and he was ready for the evening. He was constantly running from something, maybe his own self, maybe death.

The bruin won the hockey game, and we felt like kings, as if we had punched death itself in the face. We devoured the sweetness of Freyy like Freeman devoured alcohol – with joy and without thought.

"Now we're going to a restaurant, boys, my treat!" Frey shouted.

He had grown a mustache for the occasion, and he had something wild in his eyes, he looked unpredictable. Dress shirt, two buttons undone, dress shoes. It was as if he wanted to fool the world that he had class.

"Okay, but I'm holding back tonight," said Freeman.

There was no restaurant, Frey changed his mind, nor did he treat us to anything. It became a drinking spree instead. Bitter crusade drunkenness and women's rejections. We stopped at every bar we happened to cross paths with. We were like a pack of hungry wolves, ready to devour the meat the city threw at us. Freeman was completely gone, appalling, wet shirt from drinks he had spilled, snot had run from a nostril. The people around us observed us with both disgust and envy, for they knew we were living, really living.

"What the hell, how about some tequila?" wondered Frey.

"NO," shouted Freeman, "no tequila for me, I have to hold back."

"But just a little one?" tried Frey.

"I SAID I'M HOLDING BACK," shouted Freeman.

"But you'll have one, right Hilding?" asked Frey.

"Of course," I said.

"I CAN'T GET IT UP," shouted Freeman, "I CAN'T FUCK!"

Frey and I looked at each other, searching for words, but found none.

"That's why I'm holding back," said Freeman and released what seemed to be weeks of pent-up tears.

"There, there... I bet you can fuck," said Frey.

"No, I can't, I can't get it up," sobbed Freeman.

"There, there, buddy. One day at a time," said Frey, placing a comforting hand on his shoulder.

We drank in bars, we danced, we fought, we loved, and we hated.

"I think I need to head home," I said.

I took the night bus home, over an hour's bus ride. I fell asleep on the bus and then passed out as soon as I got home. My bed was mat on the floor.

It was around 1 PM, and I got dressed to head out into the city's jungle again. I was restless, hungry for more, for a continuation of what we had started the night before.

I met up with Frey downtown. We had coffee at a café, as if we were ordinary people, as if we hadn't run through the night like wild animals just a few hours earlier.

Then we headed to Frey's hotel. It had seen better days. But it didn't matter, we weren't there for comfort, we were there to live and die. We drank beer and waited for Freeman; he was as much a part of this story as we were. Then we would go to a nightclub, where we would dance and sing and laugh and cry together until we could no longer distinguish between reality and dream. I opened the first beer. A brew that tasted of mold and freedom. It was a taste that was hard to describe, but I knew I would never get enough of it.

Freeman arrived at the hotel after a while. We played some songs from the phone, old hits from a time better than our own, and drank a few beers. Frey was hungry, so he suggested we eat somewhere before heading to the nightclub. Frey doesn't take no for an answer, so we went out into the raw evening to find a place to eat. Our steps echoed against the cold cobblestones as we settled for a place that I don't remember the name of.

Next to us, a couple was making out. It felt like they were seconds away from full-blown intercourse. We watched intently, like voyeurs, waiting for the moment he would whip it out.

"That's the closest we'll get to anything tonight," I said.

"Speak for yourself, I'm jerking off when I get home," Freeman said.

After the meal, we headed to the nightclub. There was something in the air, something that drove us forward, something that said this was a night that shouldn't be lost. We roamed around inside like restless spirits, looking for some kind of action, anything that could keep death at bay.

"How long until this guy gets thrown out?" I asked the bouncer, pointing at Freeman.

"1 hour and 20 minutes?" Freeman guessed himself.

I noticed a woman. She seemed to radiate light in the darkness, like a star that had fallen to earth or some bullshit like that. She had tied a shirt over her stomach and had all the buttons unbuttoned. Big juicy bosom. I could have loved those tits. Many guys approached her, but she just played with them, like a cat with a mouse.

"She sucks a mean dick," Freeman said, nodding at her.

The guys were all over her, they looked sick, crazy. They wanted to see more, they wanted to see everything.

"She has sucked cock before, you know that. And it might happen again," continued Freeman.

The aforementioned bouncer threw us out onto the filthy streets of Boston. Mostly because Frey fell asleep. That's what happens when you have a job and get into that death routine that sucks the life out of your poor soul.

"I'm craving something light, moose meatballs or something," said Frey. "I don't want anything, come to think of it, I just want to fuck," he continued.

Shortly after 5 AM, I was in bed, and I seemed to have survived, against all odds. I had run out of breakfast, so I had to go to the grocery store as soon as I woke up. With heavy steps, I headed there. A beggar wanted money, as if he was the only one going through hell. An old lady was blocking the bananas, as if she was God's own messenger, there to pick a bunch of bananas. An old man drove his shopping cart into my legs, like a symbol of life's pain and something else I didn't know what it was.

Everything felt so intense on days like these. It was as if life was a circus, and I was the main act. But I could never perform in the way the surroundings hoped and demanded. I exchanged some pleasantries with the cashier who probably hated me. The banana-blocking old lady continued with the same theme and blocked the exit. The beggar wanted his money, but I still had none.

SISYPHUS

My first gig as a gardener for the upper-class snobs was to weed the flowerbed for a family in Brookline, the promised land, where success and well-being awaited around every corner—at least according to those who had never had any contact with reality.

I rang the bell. I was ready for a bitter hag who looked down on people like me, who came from the slums, unshaven, rough-around-the-edges workers. I was ready for the Countess of Habsburg with a plate of cucumber sandwiches and a self-help book, sitting in the picturesque garden while the Indian servant brought out lemonade. But the woman who answered was just a normal damn person.

I got down on all fours in the flowerbeds and tried to fool myself and her into thinking I knew what the hell I was doing. I didn't have a good grasp on what was a weed and what was a flower, but I sounded confident when she went over what I was supposed to do. I lulled her into a false sense of security, then took wild guesses at what to pull and what to leave. After two hours, she came out again.

"Oh my god!" she exclaimed.

That's it, I thought. Short career, fired after one day.

"You're doing such a great job!" she continued.

I thanked her and tried to figure out if she was joking or serious.

I went to the next gig, where I would humiliate myself by hauling six tons of soil up a hill, with nothing but a spade and a wheelbarrow. After playing Sisyphus with the soil, I was to cut some branches from a birch tree. The old man who ordered the job sat on his walker right by the tree, like a perverse spectator, enjoying every drop of sweat that ran down my forehead.

I had asked for a ladder to reach the branches, but all he had to offer was a rickety, moldy chair from a time when dance bands were popular. The chair was naturally too low, so I had to balance myself like a circus artist on it and stretch to reach the branches with the chainsaw. The old man got one of the branches on him, knocking him off his walker.

"'SNAILS," he shouted.

I pulled the branch away and helped him up.

"You alright?" I asked.

"It takes more than a little branch to send Theodore to his grave," he said, looking more alive than before. But I knew better—it was a near miracle he survived. Just inches away from getting the branch right in the noggin, and he would have kicked the bucket then and there, the old bastard.

I sawed off the last branches, then Theodore's wife came out, a woman who looked like she would rather be somewhere else than with Theodore. But that's life, you don't always get to choose. She handed me a beer, and I couldn't help but think she might want me instead of Theodore.

"Do you like beer?" she asked, and I couldn't help but smile. What kind of question is that? It's like asking if you like breathing.

"Sure," I said, taking it.

"Good! I don't like beer myself," she said and winked at me, as if it was something to be proud of.

"Yeah, who the hell doesn't like beer," Theodore said.

I trudged off toward the train with the beer in my hand, it was hot as hell and a cold beer was just what I needed. It felt good to be heading home, or perhaps more importantly, away from Theodore.

The next day, I forced myself out of bed at 6 AM. An idiotic time to wake up, but what can you do? I had to get to the office to meet my colleague for the day, Pekka. Together we'd take a company car out to where the customer of the day lived.

I left the apartment and pressed the elevator button. The elevator was our only access to a mirror, so I brought some wax and had the time between the seventh floor and the ground floor to do something decent with my hair. I reached the ground floor and realized I'd botched my hair, so I went back up to grab a cap.

Pekka, the Finnish swine, was waiting for me when I arrived. He looked as worn out as I felt, and there was something comforting in that. We immediately headed to the villa. The hedge was three meters high, with no visibility. There were Italian arches and marble everywhere. Seven tons of gravel lay on the driveway.

"This needs to be spread out over the entire path up to the house," said the prima donna who lived there.

"Five centimeters thick," she continued, then drove off.

Pekka and I grabbed a wheelbarrow each and started shoveling. I worked like a madman, wanting to get the crap done and then head into town for a cold beer. The sun was merciless, as if God Himself had decided to punish us sinners.

"Shall we take a coffee break?" Pekka asked, and when a Finn named Pekka suggests a break, you don't argue. We jumped in the company car and sped off to a gas station.

"It's like a sauna in here," Pekka said with his Finnish accent. "Not that I mind a sauna... Do you like saunas?" he continued.

"Yeah, it's relaxing," I said.

"I'm from Finland, we love saunas," Pekka said, as if his accent hadn't already given that away.

We each bought ourselves a cup of tired old coffee. While we sat there drinking our coffee, Pekka kept talking about Finland, saunas, and the whole damn package.

We headed back to the villa and resumed shoveling gravel. We had made good progress. It was only 10 o'clock, and we were close to done. I felt relieved but also a bit worried about what Pekka would think of it. He struck me as a man who never knew when to stop working and start living. I looked up at him through a layer of dirt and sweat that insisted on attacking my eyes.

"So, what now?" Pekka said, standing on the lawn in all his glory. I stood beside him, feeling stressed. Weren't we going to leave? Pekka started rambling on, about anything and everything, roofs, trees, bushes, animals, bugs, pressure washers, saunas, everything he could think of to make time pass. He inspected the customer's pool, villa, garage, garden, the vegetation.

"Shall we go?" he finally asked. It was half past eleven.

"Fine by me," I said.

"We have to agree on how many hours to log," he said.

"Yeah, sure, what do you think?" I asked.

"Shall we say six hours?" Pekka said.

"Sound's good," I said, even though it had only taken a little over three. Those were the dirty tricks we lived for, Pekka and I.

I called in sick for the rest of the week.

ECHOES OF TRIUMPH

Gameday was here and it was time to show the rest of the world what we were made of. Freeman and I were there to witness it live. It was a Monday, but the bar was open, and the beer was inexhaustible. There was a hell of an atmosphere. We were surrounded by brothers and sisters in the fight. We screamed and sang and swore and drank, and for a moment, everything else was gone. We were linked by a shared love — The Bruins — and a common enemy — everything else.

When the Bruins scored, we exploded in cheers, and when the others did the same, we felt death's cold hand gripping our hearts. But we never gave up, not ever. And it paid off, the Bruins won 3-1. We stood and screamed, sang, and roared long after the game ended. TV interviewed Patrice Bergeron down on the ice, and he didn't hear it, but he was our king.

Freeman and I decided to let the night embrace us after the game. It was a party, and everyone was invited. We walked along tiresome sidewalks, our voices echoing between the buildings. Spring had arrived, but it felt like something else was coming, something dark, heavy, and unholy. I asked Freeman for a cigarette.

"A cigarette? You want a cigarette?" he said.

"Yes, please," I said.

"Here's your damn cigarette," he said, throwing the pack on the ground, stomping on it, and kicking it away. I went and picked it up and managed to find a cigarette that had survived Freeman's violence. Freeman snatched it from my mouth and crushed it in his hand. His eyes were dark with anger and sorrow, as if he wanted to say, "This is all we have, and it will never be enough."

"You don't smoke," he said.

We settled into the kitchen couch at the party. It was a two-room apartment, packed with germ-spreaders and fake smiles. Melody, who lived there, would pass us by now and then, eager to make sure we were comfortable.

"Everything alright?" Melody asked.

"I saw a guy with two dicks fuck a girl with two pussies once," Freeman said.

"Yeah, but are you alright?" Melody asked.

"Personally, I love dogs," I started, but Freeman interrupted me.

"I hate myself," he said matter-of-factly.

"Oh, why's that?" Melody asked with a voice that seemed to genuinely care, even though her eyes were glued to the wine glass in her hand.

"Eh, never mind, but we should probably head home," Freeman said.

It was a code word we had agreed on earlier; it meant we were going out to the pub. Come to think of it, that code word just made things worse. In Melody's eyes, we'd come to her place, sat on the kitchen couch, drank obscene amounts of whiskey and wine, only to leave for home within an hour. But maybe that's exactly what we were trying to do—make everything worse. What else was there to do?

"I am absolutely attracted to you," Freeman said to Melody before we parted ways at the front door. There was something honest about Freeman's broken soul that spoke to me. Melody's eyes lit up with that so-called despair. I stood there, laughing uncontrollably. I felt good. I was happy.

WAITING FOR SHARLEXIA

I just wanted to be a man drinking his coffee in peace and quiet, but my stomach was tied in knots. I didn't even know what she looked like; I only knew her name was Sharlexia. But even though I had never seen her, I imagined her as some sort of goddess.

"Oh god, I don't feel well," I said to Freeman.

"Why's that?" Freeman asked.

"That girl... I don't even know what she looks like," I said.

"Just have a plain cup of coffee and go home," Freeman suggested.

"Yeah… Speaking of which, I think I need a refill," I said.

"And you're hungover too," Freeman added.

"That's true," I said.

"Anyway, Sharlexia? What kind of a name is that?" Freeman said.

"I like it," I said.

"It sounds like she lives with her mom in a trailer, smoking a pack a day," Freeman said.

I headed to the subway, feeling like a prisoner on his way to the gallows. I wished I could sit around with Freeman all day, drink coffee, and escape the melancholy. I tried to read on the train, but it never works dammit. The train was, as always, full of loud damned people, each with their own wretched lives.

I stood at an intersection, waiting. My stomach ached and my knees barely held me up. She was somewhere in the crowd, laughing at me, her and her friends. I didn't know what to look for, didn't know any distinguishing features, but she knew what I looked like, she knew exactly.

I heard laughing from the crowd, they're laughing at me, but I'll show her, I'll show them all, every damn one of them, they'll choke on their damn laughter, those bastards.

"Hi," said a damn supermodel. She blinded me, her glow made the sun ashamed and hide behind the clouds. She radiated beauty, she burned fiercely, violently, intensely, no one was left untouched. I defiled this creation of God with my mere presence, like a slimy fly on a pristine white cloth. Her beauty would make Helen of Troy look like a Sunday morning after a wild Saturday night. She was the perfect dream and the worst nightmare at the same time.

I looked behind me, searching for who she could have said "hi" to, but there was no one there. I turned back, she looked me in the eyes. I pointed questioningly at myself.

"Uh, hi," I said, "Sharlexia?"

"Yes, that's me," she said.

"Nah...?" I said.

I threw my arms out, gestured for a hug. This is my only chance, I thought. Reluctantly, she gave in. We went to a café, drank coffee, and talked, but I felt out of sorts. It felt like my heart was going to leap out of my chest and scream, "Throw in the towel, you idiot!"

I drank so much coffee I spiraled into an existential crisis. Was this my body? Were these my thoughts? Where was I really? Who am I? I was dizzy.

"What would you do if you knew you were going to die tomorrow?" she asked.

"Tough question, I don't know man. Anyway, the game's about to start," I said, feeling a bead of sweat tracing down my forehead. I was having a full-blown panic attack.

I stumbled out of the place, feeling like I was going to suffocate. I headed over to Freeman's place.

The Bruins lost, making it two for two losses that day. Beaten in the quarterfinals and there was no God. I knew I would never see Sharlexia again, and I also knew she would live on in my memory as a reminder of everything I could never have.

Now there was no hockey to follow, nothing to hope for. Freeman and I decided to take a walk. We walked through rain and darkness, thinking about all the stupid things we'd done in our lives. Maybe I should have been a better person, maybe I should have treated women better, maybe I should have followed some other damn sport.

"What would you do if you knew you were going to die tomorrow?" I asked Freeman.

"Cry," he answered.

RILEY THE BON VIVANT

Calvin was originally from the Philippines. He followed a boxer from there who was one of the best in the world. "In the Philippines," he said, "everyone sits in front of the TV or radio when he has a match. The streets are completely empty, crime drops to zero."

We started boxing in a shabby basement. We needed something to do to numb the feeling that life was going to hell, and what better way than to hit something until your knuckles bled? It was a cramped place with a low ceiling, worn-out floor, shabby walls, ingrained sweat. There were a few women training there too. One woman looked particularly good, and my eyes kept getting drawn to her, and I hated it, and I hated myself for it. She moved in the ring with precision and power that made me want to throw in the towel.

Drinking, writing, and boxing, those were three simple things, no drama, just the way I liked it. But that desire kept creeping in. Sex was all well and good, but perhaps a relationship too. Kids, a nice apartment, a bed, clean dishes, a couch, a TV, a variety of potholders. I wanted kids, I was starting to mature, it was time to stop drinking, start keeping up the house, doing the dishes, cooking. Women represented that to me, a decent life, a practical life. They were like angels coming to save me from myself and the mistakes I'd made over the years. But it also meant a lot of drama, if experience had taught me right. That life wasn't meant for me, an alcoholic, an idiot, a living cliché.

It was Easter and we needed to celebrate. Calvin, Freeman, and I were caught in a three-day whisky-fueled whirlwind that would probably drag us to some bottomless abyss. But hell, it was Easter. We ended up at a party at one of Freeman's many girlfriends, Camilla's, place. That's where we met Riley, a guy who struck me as a real bon vivant, at least if your hobby is drowning little kittens. Before the whisky hit, I blushed like a schoolgirl every time he opened his mouth and spewed something nasty.

"I work part time," Freeman said.

"Part time!? You can't live on a part-time salary," he bellowed, as if Freeman's life choices were a personal insult to him.

We thought he had swiped Freeman's beer, but we couldn't be sure, so we snooped around the apartment, trying to gather evidence. We found one of Freeman's bottles close to Riley's seat, and that was all the proof we needed. We took a few of Riley's bottles from his bag in the fridge, as cowardly and sneaky as we accused him of being. He didn't notice because he was busy trying to impregnate a woman in the host's bedroom. Maybe she was his sister, maybe she was his mother. What do I know? I didn't care.

We hit the bar and settled into a booth instead of wandering around like restless spirits.

"Is this seat taken?" a Swedish blonde asked.

"Nope," Calvin said.

Then her grubby (male) friends crawled out of the shadows and joined us.

"I've been to LA and New York," said the blonde, who was 50% boobs. "Are you drinking wine? That's gay," she continued, directed at Freeman. Freeman, who was still agitated from Riley, shot back immediately,

"Oh, so you've managed not only to buy a plane ticket but also to get on and off a plane."

She didn't know how to respond, so he continued his verbal assault,

"You sound like a farmer," he said. She really wanted to sleep with Freeman after that.

The bar closed and we headed outside. Calvin took a piss on a pile of newspapers outside a hotel.

"Don't do it," Freeman said.

"Do it," I said.

"Why do they call you Freeman anyway?" Calvin asked.

"Because you're a whore," replied Freeman.

I woke up from a dream where I was a hero, the ruler of everything. I stood at the edge of a pier, pissing like a king. But as soon as I opened my eyes, I realized I was just Hilding, a pathetic drunk who had soaked his own mattress in piss. I thanked my lucky stars that I didn't have a woman besides me. She would have told the whole world about Hilding, the bedwetter, and how he turned their romantic night into a nightmare. Maybe she would have written a book about it. Maybe it would have become a bestseller that took her to the fancy salons.

Easter is a time of suffering, so I stayed in my piss bed for over an hour. Finally, I decided to face the day, head-on. Freeman was sprawled out on his filthy mattress. It was three o'clock, so I gave the mattress a loving kick.

"Aren't you going to get up you old piss drunk?" I said.

He was drunk and had no idea where or who he was. Fuck him, I headed for the train to go see Calvin instead. The train was packed, people everywhere, all eager to get somewhere or maybe flee from something. I had to stand by one of the doors, and it smelled like shit. All these damn animals acting on instinct. One station later, a mother with her stroller got on. She looked at me like I was something she scraped off her shoe. She saw me for what I was—an incompetent loser. I feared her. Her hatred was also sexy somehow. As a captivating mixture of risk and pleasure.

Calvin knew a good burger joint, so we went there. We drank beer and ate burgers, and I was starting to feel real good. Easter is a time of resurrection.

SOBER WEEKEND BLUES

Mom was visiting me and Freeman over the weekend, which meant a sober weekend. The last thing I needed.

We were at an art museum. The paintings had messy lines all over. They reminded me of when the cat accidentally stepped in its own shit and ran across the floor in panic. I didn't get it, but what do I know about art?

Some fat guy caught my attention. He wore a T-shirt with the Budweiser-logo. If his body was any clue, he loved that beer. He'd slipped into that T-shirt in the morning and then swaggered off to Prince Eugen's highly esteemed museum. Maybe he'd gotten lost on the way to the bar. He didn't fit in among the society folks there, and he didn't give a damn. This man knew what he wanted. A true ambassador for Budweiser. And it sure worked on me.

Other visitors with well-groomed hair and fortunes that exceeded the point where money mattered looked at him with a mix of disgust and curiosity, as if he were an annoying stain someone had scribbled on a Monet. He stopped in front of a painting, a beautiful scene with heavenly angels and gods. He stood there for several minutes, maybe trying to understand what was so special about it. The truth is, he was more real than any of those angels would ever be.

We went to the café and bought tea. Shortly after we sat down, two women who stood out from the other guests arrived. They were my age, they looked good, and they knew they looked good. Their tits spilled over the table, their dresses struggling to contain them. Suddenly, I felt like having a snack with my tea.

They sat there with their big bosom, like they belonged to the seven wonders of the world, and thought they had something on me. But they were too fat for me. I could do better than that. I wasn't the kind of man to fall on my knees and beg for mercy just because some tits danced in front of me.

"What the hell are you staring at? Want to touch or something?" she said.

"Staring?" I scoffed, then quickly scurried away.

We left the museum and walked around the streets downtown. I was tired, irritable, full of hate. Ugly buildings loomed on either side, ugly buildings with ugly people inside, and I'd slept too little for too long. Sad violin notes filled the square, feeding the depression. What would I ever become? Who was I fooling? I couldn't write, didn't want to work, didn't want to study, just wanted to drink. Society wasn't made for me, the gutter was my future. The gutter, wearing a beer T-shirt.

MASTER OF DESTRUCTION

Monday, damn Monday. I had to work. Five hours in Belmont, an hour's commute each way. I felt like an alien out there among the luxury houses, SUVs, hedges, lawns, and Botoxed housewives. I always longed to return to Dorchester. To the slums, public transit, communal patios, that neighbor blasting crap music around the clock. I wanted culture clashes, language clashes, a diversity of voices and faces: Spanish, Russian, Finnish, Arabic, Persian, English. I wanted pickpockets, beggars, and the raw, pulsing atmosphere. It wasn't pretty, but it was home, and I didn't want to trade it. In Dorchester, you didn't need to comb your hair or iron your shirt.

I rang the doorbell. A voice echoed from an open window upstairs. "I'm coming," it shouted. After a while, a man in his 40s opened the door.
"Hey, hi," he said.
"Hi, Hilding," I said, grabbing his outstretched hand.

"Stanley," he said.

He had only one sock on, a bathrobe, messy hair, unshaven.

"Had a bit too much gin and tonic last night," he said. "I blame the neighbor."

"Yeah, it happens," I said.

"A bit of Tuesday drinking, or what day is it?" he asked.

"It's Monday," I said.

"Oh, Sunday drinking then. Come in, come in, I'll get you some coffee," he said.

I sat at the kitchen table and waited. Stanley was still drunk and reeked of booze.

"Lucky my wife isn't at home, she wouldn't have let me fuck for a month," he said.

He brewed us some coffee and then he sat down across from me.

"Nice house, nice area," I said.

"Yeah, it sure is, but it comes at a price," he said.

"Yeah, of course," I said.

"This damn house gave me a breakdown," he said.

"That's rough," I said

"But you haven't had it easy either, right?" he wondered.

"Maybe not, but who has?" I said.

"We're not so different, you and I," he said.

Personally, I searched long and hard for any similarities. He was nice, but there was something about him that scared me. Was I afraid of becoming him? He had a ravaged look, a face that bore the marks of hundreds of sleepless nights and thousands of meaningless days.

"You look like a creative person," he said. "Are you?"

"I don't know, I write," I said.

"I can tell. I paint myself. Want to see some paintings?" he said.

We went to the living room. It was messy everywhere, paper covering all the floors because he was in the middle of renovating the house when he hit the wall. It was cluttered with boxes, clothes, shoes, kitchen items, bathroom items, and cleaning supplies. The paintings were on the floor, leaning against a wall. He picked up painting after painting, explaining what he meant with that line, that stroke, that symbol.

"It's emotions," he said.

"You have a lot of emotions," I said.

I walked to the door, ready to get started in the garden.

"I should get to it," I said.

"Borrow my boots if you want," Stanley said.

"No, it's fine, I have work shoes," I said.

"Do as you wish, but I think it's better if you take them," he said, handing them over. He seemed like the kind of guy who needed to do someone a favor, so I slipped them on.

Outside, the rain was pouring down and the wind was whipping my face. The list of things to do in Stanley's garden was long. It was one of those days, gray, dreary, overcast, cold, no woman, and the rain felt fitting. The kind of rain that does its best to ruin everything in its path.

Stanley wanted me to move two small cherry trees. I explained it would probably kill them, but he didn't care. I started digging around the first one. I hit a stone, lifted it away, and displaced a dozen beetles. I accidentally killed a few with the spade—it was a full-on war in Stanley's garden. One beetle wanted revenge, a big bastard, coming at me full of hate, determined to kill me like I'd killed its firstborn. The flame of vengeance and justice burned in its eyes. I put the spade in front of it, thinking I could carry it away, but it was sly, stayed still, tried to make itself invisible, it had patience. It was also gross, and I felt uneasy. Stanley, blissfully unaware of the war in his garden, came out with a cup of coffee in hand.

"It's looking good," he said, as if it was any comfort when you're fighting for your life.

I shoved the spade into the ground and saw I'd accidentally split a worm in two. A horrific way to die.

I remembered the beetle, which I'd forgotten about. I scanned the ground around me, but it was gone. I was their worst enemy that day. It was our Waterloo, and it wasn't me who came out Freyious, it was the goddamn spiders. I saw one of those black quick bastards skittering across the ground in front of me. I recoiled, and we danced together on the battlefield, the spider and I, like two old enemies who couldn't help but hate each other.

"My best advice I can give you is to seek help," Stanley said like some wise man on a mountain.

What the hell is he talking about, I thought, as I kept an eye on the spider and tried to stay away.

"You know what I'm talking about," Stanley said. "The addiction issues."

It's you who has problems, you damn lunatic, I thought. The spider had stopped, right next to one of the cherry trees. I spotted a spider on the trunk too. I followed the trunk with my eyes up to the crown. The tree was swarming with spiders, every branch, twig, and leaf housed a spider. They did everything to mess with me. I panicked and jumped back. I wanted to burn the whole damn tree down.

"It's genetic," Stanley droned on.

Shut the hell up, Stanley. Then suddenly, a spider dropped from the brim of my cap, dangling right in front of my eyes. I screamed out loud and swatted at it. My pulse raced, and I turned pale, like I'd stared death in the face. The spider was gone, but where? Meanwhile, Stanley kept on telling me who I was.

"It's true," I said, just to make him shut up.

"I've seen a lot of shit," he said and continued, "but I'm not whining about it. Like those damn immigrants."

It was only a matter of time before Stanley played that old card. He was as predictable as a bad novel, and I was tired of listening.

"They just whine, don't they?" he said.

"I don't know, I don't care," I said.

I grabbed the spade and started digging again, from an angle that didn't make me vulnerable to spider attacks.

"You don't care!? They've practically taken over the country," Stanley said.

"As long as I can screw, drink, and write, they can take over whatever the hell they want. When did everything else get so damn important?" I muttered.

I slog through that Monday, my hands covered in soil and my heart shrouded in sorrow. The master of death and destruction—that's what I was. When I returned to Dorchester, it was like a heavy burden lifted from my shoulders. I stepped off the bus and took a deep breath of the fresh, polluted air that embraced me with love and understanding. It was good to be home. No spiders, no luxury villas, no snobs.

FREEMAN'S DESCENT

I stepped out of my room. Freeman was sitting on the couch, staring blankly at the wall. He was a sorry sight. Drinking whisky straight from the bottle. And not just any whisky, my whisky!

Once he drank from a glass, but he couldn't be bothered to wash them up anymore, he couldn't be bothered with anything anymore, he was depressed, life had stormed and thundered at him lately, attacked and forced itself upon him. The bottle was his best friend and only solace in a world where everything else seemed to have abandoned him. Or maybe there was nothing wrong with the world, just with him. But who was I to judge? I was a drunk too.

I sat down next to him on the couch, grabbed the whisky bottle, and took a hefty swig.

"I had a dream of becoming a writer, but everything I write is crap," Freeman said.

"Come on, that story about the guy jerking off was good," I said.

Freeman shook his head and told me about a dream he had.

"I dreamed of something I wanted to turn into a story. I became obsessed, I wrote day in and day out. I poured my soul into that damn story, and I kept dreaming about it, night after night. It was like God Himself guided my hands to create something beautiful. Finally, it was finished, and you know what? It was pure crap," Freeman said.

We drank in silence for a while, staring at the wall, like madmen. Freeman cleared his throat, as if gathering courage to say something he'd been carrying for months.

"Girls are... I'm scared of girls," he said. "They're deeply loving, but then they want to fuck like hell too."

"Yeah, I guess. How are you holding up buddy?" I said.

"They lie and cry to Titanic, then want to ride dick for hours. Explain that?" he said and started laughing hysterically, as if he had just told the best joke in the history of the world.

He had really changed, and not in a good way. He drank all the time, and I couldn't remember the last time I saw him sober.

"Cheers, you cocksucker," he said.

He took a swig of whiskey, then smashed the bottle against the doorframe. His whole being screamed that the world owed him something, and it was time to collect.

"Whores," he yelled and lunged at me. He pressed the sharp remains of the bottle against my throat.

"I am death, and hell follows me," he said.

He sat over me for a while, his eyes black holes sucking in all light and hope. I thought about my lovely little spot and longed for it to be over. Suddenly he got up and sat down on the couch, as if nothing had happened.

I lay on the floor, soaking in the lovely atmosphere for a while. After the shock wore off, I decided to get out of the apartment. Freeman was drinking from a newly opened bottle of brandy. His face twisted into a strange smile, his eyes still dark as night. I sneaked past him.

I went to the local café. I met two guys who looked at me as if I were a monkey that accidentally dressed in human clothes. I probably couldn't live with Freeman any longer, the old drunk. I had moved ten times in a year, what's an eleventh. I never identified with my home, like women do.

I went down to the pub and had three good beers. I looked for the woman who would save my poor soul, but she must have gotten lost on the way. Or maybe I was the one lost. Like a summer cat left to its fate at the summer cottage, while the merciless winter was rolling in. I went home and snuck in, hoping Freeman had passed out. He was sprawled on the floor. I stepped over him and went into my fantastic room where the lamp lacked a shade, the mattress had piss stains, dust bunnies carried ape fever, and the window showed the best sides of Dorchester. I grabbed my revolver under the pillow and said a silent prayer to a God I never believed in that I wouldn't have to use it.

CHELSEA'S SECRET

I woke up to birdsong outside the window. She was already awake, watching me.

"Creepy," I said.

"Want breakfast?" She asked.

"No thanks," I said.

"Coffee?" She asked.

"If you insist," I said.

She got up and went to the kitchen. I realized I was naked, so I grabbed my boxers. I sat on the edge of the bed, trying to remember who this woman I had woken up with was. I went to the front door and opened it to check the name on the door. Lily Evans.

"Don't you ever feel any positive emotions?" Lily asked from the kitchen.

"What do you mean?" I asked, walking into the kitchen. Lily was sitting at the kitchen table with a cup of coffee. I poured myself one and sat down opposite her.

"You said last night that you don't. I mean what about love?" Lily said.

"Love is a worthless feeling. Related to anxiety, I think," I said.

"For me, love is important, it feels like love helps me through my days. All kinds of love, big and small," Lily said.

"Yeah, I don't know. I don't want to die. I just don't want to live. Kidding. I'm just lost at the moment. I'm wandering aimlessly, no goals, no direction. I try different things but don't even know what I hope it'll lead to. I have only a few fuzzy biological goals, like 'have sex', 'be liked', and so on," I said.

"Well, you fulfilled one yesterday then," Lily said, smiling.

I smiled back and then checked the time, which Lily noticed.

"When do you have to be at work today?" she asked.

"By 9, I have a meeting," I said.

"Okay, you can ride with me," Lily said, and so we headed to work.

Lily parked outside my office. I grabbed my work bag that I'd lugged around all evening and got out of the car.

"Thanks for the ride," I said.

"Hilding?" Lily said.

"Yeah?" I said.

"Why do you want to piss on life before you've even lived it?" Lily said.

"Calm down with the spiritual stuff," I said and closed the door.

I swiped my card to get into the office, then went straight to the coffee machine to try to ease the hangover.

"Good morning, Hilding!" I heard Buckley say.

"You're coming to the meeting, right? I have big news," Buckley said.

"Of course," I said.

I grabbed my coffee cup and went to my barren office. It was completely soulless, just like me. I started the computer, then headed to the conference room for the meeting.

"Today we have a new colleague. Everyone, say hello to Chelsea," the boss said.

"Hello Chelsea," the whole team chimed in unison.

She was beautiful, piercing blue eyes, well-groomed but with something secretive, something not meant for the world to know. She carried an intense compassion, and it was clear it had cost her something. I was sold right away, damn. I wanted to know her secret. She was abstinent, reserved. Those blue eyes saw right through me, she knew what she was dealing with. These sheep's clothing fooled no one, here was a pig. A pig in sheep's clothing.

"At this meeting, I want us to talk about our values," the boss said, and I heard someone sigh.

"Don't blame me, this comes from higher up. So, what do we think is important for us as a team?" the boss continued.

"I think it's important that we are happy and kind to each other," said one of those pompous bastards who wanted a promotion.

"I think the holidays are important. And the coffee machines," said the clown.

The boss's phone rang.

"I have to take this call, so we'll end the meeting now. Think about this, and we'll revisit it at our next meeting. Unless anyone has anything else?" the boss said.

"Can I just add something?" Buckley asked.

"Of course," the boss said, pointing at him.

"It's just that I've been to the doctor and got a diagnosis. Actually, two diagnoses. Autism and ADHD," Buckley said.

"Yippee!" exclaimed someone.

"Okay. Did anyone else have something to add? No? Then we'll wrap it up here," the boss said and left the room.

I quickly made my way to my office, the hangover gripping me hard. I saw the others shake hands with Chelsea. I had the feeling I'd seen her somewhere before.

At lunch, I sat down in the break room next to Buckley, who immediately started talking about some tedious bullshit. A girl he matched with on Tinder, who he was now warning me about.

"She's psycho," he said.

"Go on," I said.

"I went to her place, half-mast the whole way. Happy as a clam, despite the rain whipping my face, and I had no raincoat either. Once there, I rang the bell, and she opened the door. I started to unbutton my jacket, but she stopped me. 'You don't need to take it off, I just wanted to see what a real damn loser looks like,' she said and slammed the door," Buckley recounted. It was a delightful story that lifted my spirits, and I was thankful Buckley had chosen to share.

I glanced at Chelsea, she was sitting with some women and seemed to have found her place in the group. I wondered what she did in the evenings. I saw a ring on her finger. It was a shame, because there was something about her that wasn't easily forgotten. She had a flirty demeanor, and I wasn't the first or last man to think it meant something. It didn't help that I was horny as a wild animal. I had decided to stop masturbating on a strange winter evening, an evening when my psyche had combined feelings of brutal anxiety and spiritual inspiration. An evening when the pain was at its worst. An evening when I hadn't slept for two days and hadn't eaten for three.

It was like going through a second puberty. Erections at inappropriate times, feverish nights, even my voice changed. Even though the wind tormented me out on the unexplored plains, I saw something amusing in it all. We can make stones talk to each other, but the universe can make a lump of flesh think. Call it God's plan, call it chance, call it whatever you want, but this lump of flesh in our skulls can understand its surroundings, figure things out, math, biology, physics, language. It can visualize the future, remember the past, it is self-aware. But all it wants to do is fuck. I find that very entertaining.

"Any comments on that?" Buckley asked.

"She sounds like a girl with her head screwed on right. What's her name?" I said.

"Watch out for her. I'm warning you, she's crazy," Buckley said.

"That's the eighteenth woman you've warned me about. You just want them all to yourself, don't you?" I said.

I went to the coffee machine for a refill. On my way there, I saw out of the corner of my eye that Chelsea got up from her group. I punched in black coffee on the machine while humming Kumbaya.

"Hey," I heard from behind. I turned around and met Chelsea's gaze.

"Hey," I said, immediately getting a hard-on. I shoved a hand into my pocket and grabbed my penis to hide it.

"We're in the same team, right?" Chelsea asked.

My gaze wandered down, to her chest, then further, to her stomach and thighs. I wasn't the one in control anymore.

"Yes, exactly, I don't know if I've welcomed you, so welcome! How do you like it here?" I finally said.

"Thanks! I like it here, there are so many fun colleagues," Chelsea replied. She didn't seem to notice my sick behavior.

"Glad you like it, you seem like a nice person," I said while my eyes wandered up and down her body.

"Thanks, same to you... well, coffee then," Chelsea said and walked away.

I went to my office and closed the door behind me, then sat down and let my face fall into my hands. I was ashamed, what had I just experienced?

The next day, Chelsea was sitting alone in the break room when I got to work, and I felt nervous but also excited. I didn't know why; it wasn't like I stood a chance in hell.

"So, it's just us today?" I said.

"Seems like it," Chelsea replied.

"So, is everyone sick, or what's going on?" I asked.

"Yeah, I think many are working from home too," Chelsea said

It was time to take the conversation to the next level, and panic started to set in. That ancient fear of running out of things to talk about and all you can do is sit there in silence. Beads of sweat trickled down my forehead, I didn't stand a chance. I grabbed a cup of coffee and set off to my office instead. Chelsea turned and looked at me. I smiled but got no reaction. Why do you always have to do those silly damn smiles, you damned clown, I thought.

"But two of the best are here at least," Chelsea said cheerfully.

"Wow, what a compliment," I said.

"No, I mean Peter from IT, I saw him earlier," Chelsea joked.

"So, any plans for the weekend?" I asked.

"Riley will be away all weekend, so I'm alone. Cleaning and laundry, I guess. How about you?" Chelsea said.

"I'll probably do what I love most. Day drinking," I said, miming pouring alcohol into my mouth.

I had returned to the table and sat down next to her.

"Peter from IT, he's a character," I said.

"He is?" Chelsea said.

"Yeah, a contemporary character anyway. All the real characters have more or less disappeared. You know, all the sexists, all the closet alcoholics, all the untreated psychotics, all those who listen to bands like Rammstein. Yeah, the real people of the world, where have they gone?" I said.

"Maybe they got the help they needed," Chelsea said.

"Hey!" I heard someone shout. I knew who it was, but still hoped I had misheard the voice. But it was indeed Buckley, the damn swine.

"Hi!" Chelsea said cheerfully.

Buckley sat down at our table.

"Damn, Hilding, you know Peach?" he said, as if he didn't talk about her several times a day.

"Yeah?" I said.

"I saw her downtown yesterday. She smiled at me. With her whole mouth, she showed her teeth and everything. It feels strange to even think about it now, but I know it happened. And you should know that I've ejaculated at the mere fantasy of being with her. I didn't even touch the penis," Buckley said.

"Why? Why do I need to know that?" I asked.

"Well, biologically speaking, isn't it fascinating?" Buckley said, looking pointedly at me and then Chelsea, who nodded.

"Yeah, I don't know, it's probably rare," Chelsea said.

I imagined Buckley ejaculating to a fantasy about Chelsea and felt both sick and sad. Sad, because I realized that there was a man who came both from and in Chelsea, and that man wasn't me. Thank God that man wasn't Buckley either, which was a comfort.

"So, are you going to the hockey game this weekend?" Buckley asked.

"What the hell do you know about hockey?" I asked.

"I've started to appreciate hockey lately. The tackles bothered me at first, but then I learned to like it. I think the fights are ridiculous though," Buckley said.

"The tackles didn't bother you because you're a good person. They bother you because you've never felt like a real man. Macho stuff triggers your inferiority complex," I said. Buckley started humming a Bruins song.

"What complexes do you have then?" Chelsea asked.

"Do you assume everyone has complexes?" I asked.

"No, just you," Chelsea replied.

It was getting too personal, so I stood up from the table to head to my office.

"I don't have any damn complexes," I said. I wasn't going to let Buckley ruin hockey for me.

THE THEORY AND THE EVIDENCE

Freeman, Calvin, Charlie, and I were at a gathering. Strange folks, and we fit right in. A few beers deep, Sheena gestured for me to come to the bathroom. She pulled me in and locked the door.

"Want some?" she said, pulling out a bag of white powder.

"Probably not," I said.

In classic movie cliché fashion, she lined up two lines on the toilet lid. She even had a special purpose straw, which she handed to me. I took the straw and snorted one line, then passed the straw to her.

"Both are for you," she said.

I snorted the other one, stood up and leaned against the sink. She pressed herself against me and started making out with me.

"I haven't ejaculated in 40 days," I said.

She looked offended, as if I had committed a terrible crime. She was crazy, I realized that, and I found myself suddenly in her power. She could walk out of that bathroom and say whatever the hell she wanted until the clocks stopped.

"Haven't you had sex?" she wondered.

"Well yeah, but aside from that," I said, pushing her aside to get out of the bathroom.

I sat down next to Freeman.

"Jesus spent 40 days and 40 nights in the desert. He met both God and Satan," Freeman said. I wondered if I had lost my mind.

"40?" I said.

He went back to his discussion about Bigfoot with Calvin and Charlie. They seemed skeptical, I noticed, while glancing toward the bathroom. The girl had closed the door, and the closed door reminded me of the eye of a storm.

"If so many hunters keep seeing Bigfoot, how come no one has shot or caught Bigfoot? How come we never see a really good recording with the amazing cameras we have on our phones? Or all these cameras strapped to animals and in the forest; how come none of them catch Bigfoot?" Charlie said.

"I'm with Charlie on this. Such a 'creature' should have been discovered already, if it exists," Calvin said.

Freeman stared down at his beer bottle, he was somewhere else. Now it was up to me to defend Bigfoot, and suddenly I was truly passionate about the creature, and my mission in this world was to defend it.

"There are 30,000 pumas in the USA, and hunters might encounter them maybe once in their lives, so imagine if there are only, say, 1,000 Bigfoots," I said.

"Feels like all those tens of thousands of hunters should have come across a Bigfoot carcass by now," Charlie said.

"That's exactly what's missing. A body. Everything else is there. Tracks. Sounds. Impact on nature," Freeman said, having snapped out of his trance.

"Decades have passed with millions of people moving through the woods, and not a single carcass has been preserved and studied?" Charlie said.

"Just look at all the people who disappear in the forests without a trace. Despite helicopters, massive search efforts, infrared cameras, and so on. All the technology at humanity's disposal, and still, they can't find so much as a piece of clothing," I said.

"Exactly," Freeman agreed.

"Yeah, but that's a person who might be dead somewhere, eaten by animals, or buried and hidden. Bigfoot is alive and moving around," Calvin said.

"Sure, but there's an enormous amount of land, and who knows, maybe you'd find something if you conducted a thorough search, but I don't know if that's been done. Take those who disappear; you can have the last GPS location and still not find anything, even though it might be just a few square miles. Multiply those square miles by a few hundred thousand, and you have very slim chances of finding Bigfoot," I said.

"Yeah, it's a theory, nothing that can be proven, and nothing the skeptic can conclusively disprove. All you can do is consider the 'evidence' and form an opinion on what it suggests," Charlie said.

"Yeah, I believe neither this nor that. What I see are indications that lack explanations. There's a lot that's strange, and after hearing a lecture by a renowned biologist, I'm not ready to close the book on Bigfoot," Freeman said.

"Cheers to that then," Calvin said, holding up his beer bottle.

Just as we were about to toast, the bathroom door flew open, and all eyes turned on Sheena. She pointed at me, and all eyes turned to me instead. I shrugged questioningly. With legs struggling to find balance, she made her way to me and sat on my lap. Everything played out in a haze, and it felt like everything would be okay somehow.

Minutes passed, maybe hours, and I suddenly found myself at a table in a bar.

"Peter Bjorn and John – Young Folks makes you proud to be Swedish," Charlie said.

"I thought Peter Forsberg made you proud to be Swedish?" Calvin replied.

"Well, you're wrong," Charlie answered, "how do you even come up with that whistling?"

"Jesus, I miss hockey," Calvin said.

"How about Young Folks?" Charlie continued.

"Hell, hockey has gotten me back on my feet more times than I can remember," Calvin said.

"Young Folks!?" Charlie said.

"The ref's whistle. That's something to talk about. It's pulled me out of death's grip. Lifted me from the gutter," Calvin said.

I studied Freeman. He was staring down into his beer. He lifted his gaze towards us, and it was clear he had something important to share.

"Imagine you see the light," he said.

"The light?" Calvin wondered.

"Just listen," Freeman said, and continued: "A living light so bright. Brighter than the void in the Tibetan Book of the Dead. Stronger than a thousand suns. It's beyond light, words don't suffice. And suddenly, it withdraws."

Calvin, Charlie, and I looked at each other and confirmed our confusion with a glance. We didn't know where Freeman was headed with this, but we wanted to know. He continued:

"You see a wreath of red, orange, yellow, green, blue, purple. And you see a mandala emerge. Beyond the mandala, you see black. Black like obsidian, but it's transparent. And beyond the black, you see more light, like yang for yin. And with the light comes a sound. A sound so mighty, you can't even hear it. So penetrating, you think your ears will disintegrate. Along with the colors, the sound goes down in frequency, down, down, down, until it's a low rumble vibrating so much it takes on a solid form. A spectrum of textures. All this time, you've seen this phenomenon radiate and permeate your whole being. But this is not all I can do, it says. And the light rays start to vibrate and dance like waves on the ocean, and the sound does too. And the textures start to vary in shape and color. A third dimension starts to emerge. And everything suddenly becomes much more intense," as he said this, he became more intense. He flailed and gesticulated with his arms, raising his voice.

"And everything starts to swing and flicker in all directions, and the figures you thought you could distinguish in the textures reveal more complex details you hadn't seen before, and everything is so intense, and the sound becomes so enchanting that you are no longer sure if the colors and figures can be distinguished from the sound, it's all one and the same, and you think you're going to go crazy when everything suddenly transforms into... us four, here at the table, on our chairs."

There was silence. No one quite knew what to say. It felt like I had fallen into a black hole, only to land back in the same place I was when I started falling.

Charlie took a sip of beer, then he said,

"But what about Young Folks?"

"It's Alan Watts you illiterate cocksuckers", Freeman said.

"What is this Peter Bear and John? Sounds like some dance band," Calvin said.

"Sounds like you have to work in social media and have a pilot's license for a tiny crappy plane to listen to it," Freeman said.

"You're uncultured," Charlie said.

"Cessna," I said.

"Shut up," Freeman said and continued. "I can't listen to that hipster music with my working-class background."

"How's it going with the bunny boiler?" Charlie asked, referring to Freeman's latest.

"Why is she a bunny boiler?" Freeman wondered.

"Just a feeling," Charlie said.

"It's been a while since we heard anything about her," Calvin said.

"I probably need to get out of that. It could get messy. Because we work at the same place," Freeman said.

"There are probably many couples who work at the same place," I said, thinking of a bunch of my sexy colleagues.

"Yeah, you have to find your own special way to hate each other," Freeman said, and continued:

"I saw some pictures of Ajahn Lee the other day and thought, what the hell happened? My life was nice and calm, I was going to meditate and live peacefully. After Alice, I thought I'd be single for at least 10 years."

"Try 10 days...," I said.

"A man can build dreams based on her kisses," Freeman said.

"Listen to yourself...," Calvin started, but was interrupted. An ape emerged from the shadows in the depths of the pub.

"Got a light?" he asked. His deep voice bore witness to a hard life.

"No, we don't smoke," Freeman said.

The ape looked beat-up. Scarred and tattooed arms leaned against our table. His face was tired but aggressive, and it was hard to tell if he was old or just worn out.

"I know the cops are out there, you think that's gonna stop me" he said, gesturing outside. We looked out the window but saw no one there.

"Come on, Tony, let's go," a woman our age said.

"Wow, you're cute. Your dad must be very proud of you," Freeman said, gesturing at the brute.

"That's my boyfriend," the woman said.

The orangutan took a swing at Freeman, which he dodged with little effort. I jumped up and threw a few punches at him. Before I knew it, the whole pub had grabbed him and pushed him toward the door to throw him out.

"I'm going to kill you," he yelled.

"Come at me you mongoloid! Are you fucking nuts? I eat B12 like hell! Come on, we're going to fuck you up", Freeman shouted, jumping around inside the pub.

"The biggest cockblockers in the world are the men who spread the idea that it would be slutty for a woman to fuck around," I heard Charlie say when Freeman and I returned to the table.

Sheena appeared out of nowhere and sat down at our table.

"40 fucking days?" she said.

"That's right. I don't do that stuff, I haven't ejaculated in three years, I love it, I love not ejaculating. It's the best thing I know after ejaculating," I said.

The next thing I remember is Ingrid kicking me to life on the hallway floor of her apartment.

"Good morning," she said, with a smile on her lips.

"Are you amused by this?" I asked.

"Yes," she said and helped me to bed.

Freeman was still out in the night. He had chosen to take a detour home, the dark forest path. The forest was dense on both sides, and the darkness had taken hold. Freeman went down on his knees and spread his arms, like he'd seen in the movies. Tears ran down his cheeks, but he didn't quite know why. Maybe it was for all the suffering life had in store for us artists.

He looked up at the dark sky, trying to catch a glimpse of the Andromeda galaxy that should be visible to the naked eye. Or maybe he was looking for answers. The sky, however, had none to offer, or perhaps he wasn't receptive. He woke up there in the woods some hours later, cold and miserable, his cheeks blackened. But maybe he had gleaned some kind of insight.

FAT MATS

"Think back on your life," Frey slurred between drunken hiccups.

We were sitting at his shabby two-bedroom apartment in an even shabbier neighborhood.

"All right, I like this already," I said.

He was about to go on a long rant that was going to lead to something thought-provoking. Or he was just drunk as hell.

"Your damn life," he said, taking a steady gulp.

"All the shit you've waded through, up to your damn waist in shit," he said.

"Yeah, that's true," I said.

"Not everyone would have made it through what you have," he said.

"Damn straight," I said.

"But not you. And you never complained either. So why are you so damn hard on yourself?" he said.

"Am I?" I said.

"Wouldn't it have been nice to have a friend during those rough damn times? The ones you've fought through, struggled and strived, never gave up. Maybe just a damn pat on the back now and then? An encouraging word? 'You've done a damn good job. You should know that.' And it's you who should give yourself that damn pat on the back," he said.

"Yeah, you might be right," I said.

"Yeah, it's time now. It's high time," he said and got up, heading to the kitchen. After a while, he came back with two new beers.

"Thanks," I said.

"They're for me," he said.

I fell back into my own thoughts. Frey and I didn't usually talk much, which was nice. We could coexist without unnecessary interactions.

"Are you living the dream?" I said after a while. He chuckled heartily.

"I've lived three-quarters of my life, and not an hour, not a goddamn minute, of the time I've spent doing what I wanted to do have I been paid. Forget your dreams. They'll never be anything more than just that, dreams," Frey said.

"But haven't you had fun along the way?" I said.

"You'll just become a disappointed, bitter, drunk old man. Maybe one in a million gets paid to do what they love. The rest are stuck on factory and office floors, doing the grunt work while their bodies break down year after year. But it's not those poor bastards you read about, it's some damn freak selling farts in jars for 7 000 a month you hear about. So, please, don't wait half your life to realize it was a dumb dream in a dumb world," Frey said, not having heard my question.

I said goodbye to Frey and headed downtown. Freeman had let me know he needed a drink. I just wanted to go home and sleep, but I'd also seen that Chelsea had posted stories on Instagram from a night out. I didn't even know what I'd do if I ran into her, I wasn't exactly smooth-talking. But on the other hand, anything could happen after a few drinks. God, I should know. After three units I'd fuck anything with a pulse.

I was far from enlightenment, I knew that. I wouldn't have known enlightenment if you shoved it in my face. Here, Hilding, here's the truth, you could say, and my eyes would be crossed from yet another binge. Donkeys, strivers, dogs, idiots, cooks, prostitutes, goddamn cyber bullies probably understood more than I did. But what did I care. I was in pain all the time. Once upon a time, I might have seen myself as spiritual, but it's damn easy to do that when you're feeling good. That spiritual ego can grow into a hot air balloon if you don't keep it in check. When the balloon bursts, all that's left is pain and sorrow.

I walked into a hotel downtown and bought a beer at the bar. There was something about hotel lounges. The subdued lighting, elevator music, carpeted floors, the real folks, the option to crawl up to a room if you had one too many. This hotel bar was special. They filled the beer to the brim, not to the line. Freeman walked in through the sliding doors a moment later and immediately ordered a beer.

"Alright," he said, sitting down at my table.

"Hi," I said.

"Any new miseries?" he asked.

"No, just the usual," I said.

"Have you heard of Fat Mats?" he asked.

"No, I haven't," I said.

We toasted our beers and drank a few sips in silence. Freeman looked worn out, like he hadn't slept in two weeks. I didn't have time to reflect much on that before Andrew walked into the hotel. I tried to make myself invisible, which Freeman noticed.

"What are you doing?" he asked.

I nodded towards Andrew, and Freeman turned around.

"Andrew!" he exclaimed.

Andrew came over to our table and grabbed me by the neck.

"Well, hello guys," Andrew said.

"Have you heard about Fat Mats?" Freeman asked. Andrew ignored it and focused fully on me.

"Time to cough up," Andrew said.

"What do you want me to do," I said, "you think I have cash?"

"Buy me 10 beers then, idiot," Andrew said.

"Fat Mats, you bastards, have you heard of him?" Freeman said.

Both Andrew and I turned our gaze to Freeman. Andrew let go of me and turned to Freeman, as if he were about to say something, but he couldn't find the words. I gave him a hand.

"No, tell us," I said.

"This Mats was a miner, right," Freeman said, "Now you're going to hear about this miner's gruesome fate,"

I saw Chelsea out of the corner of my eye as she walked through the entrance doors.

Chelsea grew up as a cute girl, cuter than her sister. She never felt cute herself, but everyone always told her how cute she was when she was little. Big sister got different compliments, for achievements. Chelsea always felt she was worse than her big sister because of that, and she didn't get her father's approval either. He noticed achievements, not looks.

That was my opening—women with daddy issues tended to fall for me. Chelsea had a great need for validation, but over the years she learned not to get into bad situations because of it.

She spotted me and approached our table.

"He was from Sweden," Freeman said.

"Hi," Chelsea said, looking at me.

"Hi," I said and went in for a hug.

"Good to see you," I said.

"Good to see you too. I'm going to find my friends," Chelsea said and walked away.

"Who the hell was that?" Andrew said.

"Just a colleague," I said.

"You hug all of your colleagues?" Andrew said.

"Yeah, if I meet them outside of work, sure," I said.

"She's a lesbian," said Andrew.

"Why do you think that?" I asked.

"Trust me," Andrew said.

"Should we take a shot?" Freeman said.

"Hell no," I said.

"Are you a faggot?" Andrew said.

"I don't know what to tell you, I'm just not feeling it," I said and continued, "if it were up to me, I wouldn't even be here with you right now."

"Where would you be then?" Freeman asked.

"I'd be curled up in the fetal position with my head in some woman's lap, her stroking my hair and whispering in my ear that everything is going to be alright," I said, glancing over at Chelsea a few tables away.

We drank shots and entered some kind of intermission. The atmosphere shifted to something vague. Freeman and Andrew discussed Bigfoot, and I pondered what was wrong with me, or what I had done to deserve all this crap. A pain from my back radiated towards my chest, and I hoped death had finally come to take me home.

I was stuck in a vicious cycle, thinking the universe would give me everything I wished for, any moment now. But that moment never came, and then I had worse pain and a hangover on Sunday, Monday, Tuesday, Wednesday, you name it. Then I'd realize the whole damn thing was fake, the universe wasn't going to give me a damn thing. But I let myself be fooled again and again.

Chelsea came back to our table just as Andrew was talking about his relationship problems. His partner had been unfaithful a year ago.

"I've fucked real freaks, as some kind of payback," he said.

"Hi," Chelsea said, sitting down next to me.

The pain in my back had been gradually increasing throughout the evening, becoming almost unbearable. When Chelsea sat next to me, it vanished. The best way to return the favor was probably to just leave her alone.

"Hey, having a good time?" I asked.

"Not really. It would be nicer somewhere else," Chelsea said, and I toyed with the idea that she meant alone with me somewhere.

"Where would you rather be then?" I wondered.

"Home in my bed," Chelsea replied.

"Take Hilding with you," Andrew interjected.

"He doesn't fuck, he makes loves," he continued, as if he hadn't said enough. Chelsea looked uncomfortable.

"Sorry about that guy, he's just some wino," I said quietly to Chelsea, so he wouldn't hear and interrupt more.

"Like you?" Chelsea said.

"He's right you know, but something about his wording rubs me the wrong way," I said.

"You look nice tonight," Chelsea said.

"Well, you don't stomp into the boudoir with boots on," I said.

My phone vibrated, so I excused myself to answer. I went to the restrooms to speak undisturbed.

"Hello," I said.

"I've been looking for salvation in the wrong places," Frey said on the other end.

"Really?" I said.

"I've been looking for salvation in the bottle," Frey said, and I could tell he was crying, or had been.

"I've been looking for salvation in quitting drinking too," he continued.

"You're closer than you think," I said.

"Don't be like me...," Frey said.

"What are you going to do now?" I said.

"Cry. The night is for crying," Frey said.

"Hey by the way, I don't think I can stop dreaming. I guess I'll become a disappointed, bitter, drunk old man," I said.

"Ha! You were supposed to say something along the lines of 'haven't you laughed at your job and had fun? Isn't that what we really want, just to have fun and be happy? In that case, you have been paid to do what you wanted to do,'" Frey said.

When I got back to the table, Chelsea was gone. I sat down, doing my best to play it cool.

"Sorry Hilding, your fuckdoll slipped out the door," Andrew said.

"We did our best to stop her," Freeman said.

"She's not my fuckdoll," I said.

"Your eyes were twinkling. Too bad you're so retarded. She would've been better off with me," Andrew said.

"I'm leaving now," Freeman cut in.

"What do you mean, you think im staying her with this fucking bastard?" I said.

"Where are you going? Can I come?" Andrew asked.

"Tukdam," Freeman said as we put on our coats.

"What's that?" Andrew asked.

"Meditate into death," Freeman said as we left the place.

We wandered along the streets that the night had gripped, which was their most distinctive feature.

"So, Chelsea? Is she your new target?" Freeman said.

"I don't know, she's nice," I said.

"But?" Freeman said.

"Uh, have you seen her? have you seen me?" I said.

"You shouldn't fall in love," Freeman said.

I was starting to long for a deep connection with someone. To sit across from someone and stare into each other's eyes for hours without saying a word. Or maybe just doing a bunch of different noises. It was either that or moving to a shack in the woods like the una bomber to get away from this dopamine-triggering society.

"Speaking of nothing, I meditated for an hour yesterday, sat in silence, tried to meditate into death. Kidding. But it's a whole thing in Tibet. The old monks there meditate into death. The old guard. They're tough. Then their bodies don't decompose either. It's called Tukdam," Freeman rambled, as briskly as he walked.

We walked to Frey's to check on him. We knocked gently on the door, but no one answered. The door was unlocked, so we let ourselves in. We heard Frey snoring from the bedroom.

We grabbed a beer each from the fridge and went into the living room. I sank into the couch, and Freeman stood by the window overlooking the forest.

"There's always some damn anxiety ruining all the fun," Freeman said.

"What now?" I asked.

"I've suffered and struggled. Sleepless nights leading to anxiety and depression," Freeman said.

"It's taken a toll on you," I said.

"That's good," Frey said, surprising us. He had woken up and walked into the living room with a bottle of whiskey in hand.

"There's a lot of suffering on this journey to death, and I don't think it's our job to avoid it at all costs. I think it's lessons and teachings in the underlying nature of things," Frey said.

That was enough spirituality for one night, so I decided to go home.

"The mine took his life, by the way, Fat Mats. The copper sulfate preserved his corpse, he's on display now, an attraction. That's not how you want to end up. Remember that," Freeman said as parting words.

LOSING YOURSELF

We were sitting in my car out in the woods. Chelsea was nonchalant, she couldn't give less of a damn if it was us or not, she ate people like me for breakfast. Chelsea rode me in the back seat, but it stank because I had stepped in dog shit. She put massage oil on my dick, so I didn't feel a damn thing. It was like fucking a black hole.

Her boyfriend had just gotten out of the psych ward, so he was sitting in his car outside my apartment, waiting for me. The whole story would probably end with me getting beaten black and blue, but I'm not one to live for tomorrow.

"You can't decide what pops up in your head, it's automatic processes," I said.

"But you can indulge or return to the present," Chelsea said.

"Okay," I said.

"My boyfriend is going to kill you," Chelsea said.

"This is bigger than that," I said.

I stepped out of the car and wandered into the woods. I looked back and saw the fogged-up windows and cursed the dog shit that had ruined the whole experience. I kept walking, up a hill from which I could see an open plain.

It's out on the open plains we must stand, battered and tormented. It's there we confront the truth, in all the pain, frustration, and the unknown. We can live a life in the safe, fabricated, false diversion or continue striving for what's beyond all this. Who said it was an easy truth to face? Who ever said it was easy? It's out there you must face the truth. Another second, another minute, another hour, another day.

You thought you'd get something out of all this? You wanted to become something from all this? Become what you've always wanted to be? Get what your ego craved? Newsflash, that was part of the illusion. It was what your mind wanted when it believed the illusion was real. You tried to realize the illusion by seeking the truth? Do you hear yourself, man? You're at a crossroads now, and it burdens you. It's Heavy and it's tough, and who ever said it would be easy?

You can go back to the illusion now or keep slogging toward the truth, where your heart leads you. Who said it would be easy? Who said the truth was the pretty words you always wanted to hear? Your whole life has been pretty words, and where have they taken you? To misery, fear, and destruction. You want to wake up now, but your ego thinks awakening will feed and magnify it to what it always wanted to be. Almighty. But that's not where it seems to lead you, and you're scared. Disappointed, frustrated, angry. When the truth you sought says your ego is exactly what's keeping you from seeing me, where will you go then? Back to safety, the illusion, the pretty words, lord of the hill, master, and emperor. Or will you keep striving, pushing, working your way through the thorny damn jungle? There's nothing for you beyond the next hill. After the next hill, it might be too late to turn back. Are you ready for that? Are you ready to lose yourself? Lose yourself in the truth. Your call.

We went to the pub and had a drink. The pub was full of mold, mice, and sweet talk. I wished I had met her 10 years ago and that she had given me a fair chance.

"You can't even look at me," Chelsea said.

"I never could," I said.

"Sometimes you do," Chelsea said.

I caught my reflection in a mirror at the bar. I looked like an old drunk and it seemed I had been one all my life.

"Your eyes see right through me," I said.

"Am I the bad one in our relationship?" Chelsea said.

"No, I am. It's always me, baby," I said.

"Guess what I bought," Chelsea said.

"A revolver," I said.

"No," Chelsea said.

"Maybe you should," I said.

"Because of Riley?" Chelsea said.

"Sure," I said.

"He drives 20 laps around my job every day," Chelsea said.

"Wow. I didn't even know that many laps existed," I said.

"What are we doing, Hilding?" Chelsea said.

"Don't ask me. I just feel done with this crap. Absolutely done. Tired. Not physically tired. Soul-tired. Just so damn tired. Tired of going through this, tired that nothing ever just works out. I tried. God knows I tried. It's a battle playing out in the silence between my four walls. I tell no one because who wants to be with a broken person?"

"That's when you grow," Chelsea said.

"Sure, but I don't get any insights. I just suffer like hell for a while, then it passes, and everything becomes normal again, except I'm a bit colder, a bit more dead inside," I said.

"Do you think there's something more than all this, something bigger?" Chelsea asked.

"Absolutely. The problem with you, if I may be a bit harsh, is that I don't know why I've fallen for you. I'm just one of the many guys who fall for you, and it's like you just wrap them around your finger because you need validation. You do something subtle that gets under one's skin but it's just flirting. Then you accidentally fell for me too, and maybe you'll stay with me for a while, until one day it's my turn to become Riley, because you found someone better than me," I said.

"I've bought a pair of sunglasses," Chelsea said and put them on. "How do I look?"

"You look amazing baby," I said.

If there's something bigger, some meaning to all this? One day when we're old and wrinkled and ugly, when worries have etched furrows in our brows and suffering has scorched our bodies with its terrible fire, then we will feel it. We will know it.

A DYING BREED

"Do you know who my favorite politician is?" Charlie asked.

"Austin Blair," Freeman said.

"Who the hell is that?" Calvin said while Charlie pretended to know.

"Anton Nilsson, Algot Rosberg, and Alfred Stern," Charlie said.

"I don't think they were politicians. They were terrorists," Freeman said.

"Considering you believe in Bigfoot, you're pretty cocky," Charlie said.

"Bigfoot is probably smarter than all of us," Freeman said.

"I didn't say anything about how smart he is. But yeah, he's probably smarter than you at least," Charlie said.

"Anyway, can we talk about me now?" Freeman said.

"The bunny boiler?" I asked.

"Indirectly. My dick is dysfunctioning," Freeman said.

"Maybe you're just not in the mood? She's insane," said Calvin

"Shut up, let me talk. Modern problems require modern solutions. So, I got some pills. There's a hell of a punch in them," said Freeman, taking out a package of blue pills from his pocket.

"Is that Viagra?" Charlie wondered.

"Something like that, you can fuck like beast on these bad boys," Freeman said

We laughed and talked, and our voices mingled with the jagged hum of the pub. The words blurred and the world outside felt like a distant tale. We tried to fill the void with love, Viagra, Bigfoot, and alcohol, and it worked for a while.

"Here, take one," Freeman said to me while we queued for the toilets.

"I don't need that," I said.

"You're in love, you get nervous, and then you can bet your ass the dick starts acting up," Freeman said.

"I'm not in love," I said.

"We're a dying breed, you and me," Freeman said, patting me on the shoulder.

Freeman spotted an attractive woman. He wanted to test the stuff. He took a deep breath and approached her. The rest of us watched as if it were a sport. He turned back toward us, and we nodded encouragingly.

"Can you help me test this Viagra," he thought, but the words that came out were, "Can I buy you a drink?" She nodded with a smile, and Freeman relaxed.

He needed this, someone to help him forget the bunny boiler. We also knew the chances of him finding true salvation in this pub were as slim as winning the lottery, but someone had to win. And tonight, it was Freeman's turn.

Freeman and the woman took a taxi to her place. Freeman went into the bathroom and closed the door behind him. He stood there, in front of the mirror, looking at the man staring back at him. He was no longer young, but not yet old. Though his face told stories of nights of drunkenness and days of anxiety.

He took half a pill and washed it down with water. When he came out, he found the woman sitting on the edge of the bed, her eyes glistening in the dim light.

"So, this is you," Freeman said.

"This is me," she replied.

Freeman approached her like a man who had forgotten how to walk. He trembled with nervousness and the silence was palpable. It hit him that he didn't feel anything special for this woman, and he started to regret it. But it was too late to realize that now.

He took off her pants and went down on her. She moaned and Freeman felt that he was rock hard. They completed the intercourse as if it was a job they had to do and then fell asleep.

The next day, Freeman woke up early. He got dressed and slipped out into the early morning. He realized he was still that boy who once believed in love, before the world taught him otherwise. But something inside him refused to ever give up, no matter what life threw at him.

We had planned to drink coffee and revisit last night. I couldn't help but crack a smile when I saw him approaching with dragging steps. My brother in life's battle.

"You look like you sold the butter but lost the money," I said.

"We need to get out of here," Freeman said with a pain in his voice that wasn't there during yesterday's drunkenness. "There's nothing left for us here."

We headed to a café. The wind, the sun, and melancholia kept us company.

"I feel a longing for something I can't put into words," Freeman said.

"What the hell happened last night?" I said.

"I don't want to talk about it," Freeman said.

"We keep fighting," I said. "It'll work out eventually."

We walked into a café, and it was as good a time as any for beer. I bought two at the counter and handed one to Freeman. He grabbed it and started talking about the bunny boiler.

"We've had our moments, but it never felt quite right," he said. "It's time to move on."

"Yeah, I agree, she's ruining you," I said.

We got a bit tipsy and headed to a bar instead. Outside, the rain pattered against the asphalt, and the sky didn't seem to care that we were getting wet. We walked through the heavy door of the pub, and the sound of rain gave way to lighthearted pop hits. We sat down at a table with a beer each.

"They're mixing period blood in pasta sauce now, women," Freeman said.

"What the fuck are you saying?" I asked.

"It's supposed to drive men crazy for them," Freeman said.

"Crazy for them..." I said.

Freeman gestured toward the bar.

"Look," he said.

I turned around and saw Keshani, waiting to order. I quickly turned back to Freeman.

"How do I look?" I said, brushing off my shirt.

"Repulsive," Freeman said.

We watched her receive her beer and move into the saloon. She moved with dignity, like a beautiful piece of music, and her eyes burned with mystique and secrets. She had missed us, and maybe that was just as well.

"You lose," Freeman said.

Out of nowhere, I felt a hand on my shoulder. I turned around and barely registered that it was Keshani before she was sitting in my lap.

"Hi," Keshani said, looking straight into my soul.

"Hi," I said.

I tried to think of something else to say, but the words got stuck in my throat. I couldn't shake the thought that she was just playing with me, that I was a pawn in a game whose rules I didn't understand.

Freeman extended his hand.

"Freeman," he said.

"Keshani," she said.

We got into it and talked about everything under the sun, and everything felt so right. Time passed, and the pub slowly emptied. Keshani got up from my lap.

"I like being with you," I said.

"I like being with you too," Keshani said.

She disappeared into the night that was turning into morning, and I felt empty. I didn't know if I would ever understand her, but I wasn't going to give up. Freeman and I left the pub as the morning light began to seep through the foggy windows. We walked silently beside each other, each lost in our own thoughts. The city slowly woke up, unaware of what had unfolded under the night's peculiar embrace.

"She's tricky, this Keshani. She vibrates on a damn unique frequency," I said.

"You're a smart guy," he said. "You'll crack that nut."

"How?" I asked.

"Tune your vibrations to her frequency," Freeman said. "Twiddle the controls, just do your thing, I don't fucking know."

"There's a whole undiscovered world within her, a world of beauty," I said. "I want to be part of that world. Make it our world."

"Never talk to me like that again," Freeman said.

Keshani sent a snapchat. "Thanks for tonight," she wrote.

"She writes like a retard," Freeman said.

"Shall we go back to yours and have a beer?" I asked.

"Of course," Freeman said.

We walked along the wet street when a woman's voice caught our attention.

"Hi guys," she said.

She explained she was new in town, and now she and her friend were looking for an after-party. She had that wild look in her eyes, like life had done a number on her. She and her friend danced forward, laughing loudly and drinking too quickly. We didn't know their names, but it didn't matter. They were part of the night and the chaos.

We got to Freeman's place. It smelled of stale beer and old man. We had a good time, and the conversation topics were as deep as they can be on an alcohol-soaked night. But the wolf hour can twist the best of people. The woman's laughter turned to screams. Something dark had been lurking beneath the surface, and she suddenly seemed to be fighting demons no one else could see.

"Why are you so angry?" her friend asked.

She rushed into the bathroom, where the shower dripped in a monotonous rhythm. She punched and kicked at the shower wall until it came loose. The mirror shattered, and a thousand reflections of her twisted face fell to the floor.

Freeman and I stood helpless with her friend. We didn't know whether to intervene or flee. If we hadn't been at Freeman's place, I would have bolted out the door.

Eventually, it went silent. The woman lay on the bathroom floor, surrounded by the remnants of her madness. Her breaths were the only sounds over the still music playing somewhere far away. Freeman knelt beside her.

"Are you okay?" he said.

"She can't handle her booze," her friend said.

Her friend helped her to the couch and lay down next to her. I lay on the rug in the bedroom, and Freeman in the bed. We started laughing. We laughed ourselves to sleep.

The next day, I woke up on the same rug. My whole damn body ached. But an emptiness overshadowed the pain. Why didn't I wake up next to Keshani? The smell of coffee filled the room. Freeman came in with a cup.

"Here you go, old chap," he said, handing me the cup.

Keshani had sent me a snapchat, asking me to join her at a nightclub that evening.

Evening came, and I went to the club where Keshani was. I saw her at a table with a bunch of strangers. A bunch of guys, probably named James, Michael, Riley, John, David, and William. I was too sober for that scene, so I went to the bar and bought two beers. I downed them, and then I was in a good mood. I went to the table and sat down next to some guy.

"I know a guy who's a cop," he said.

"Tell me more," I said.

Keshani spotted me and gave me a simple "hi." I felt out of place. They talked about things I couldn't relate to, so I stared off into the distance and tried to look cool. I thought I saw Keshani glancing at me out of the corner of my eye.

A band was about to play, and the group moved to the dance floor. I stayed behind, sipping my beer. Keshani emerged from the crowd and approached me. She grabbed my hand and pulled me toward the dance floor. I was properly drunk by then and had lost my bearings. We danced together, her body pressed against mine. I wasn't used to female attention, but I loved it. I hoped the damn band would never stop. But it did, and we went to a table. She took my hand under the table and began to stroke it. She really knew how to stroke a hand.

"Should we go to yours or mine?" I asked.

"Yours," she said.

"That's not an option," I said, so we went to hers.

We sat on her couch, drinking wine, as if we needed it.

"I'm going to tell secrets," I said, laughing.

I told her what people said about her behind her back and she cried. The room spun like a drunken carousel, and I couldn't even grasp why she was crying. I was praying for a moment of clarity.

"Sorry, I shouldn't have said anything," I said.

"No, you shouldn't have," she said, heading to the kitchen.

She prepared two cucumber sandwiches and then came back to the living room. She handed me one.

"Damn, cucumber sandwich," I said.

Before I could take a bite, she removed the cucumber and added an extra slice of cheese.

"Baby, tell me the worst about you," I said.

"Later, later," Keshani said, and then we fell asleep.

I woke up after what felt like an hour but was probably ten. I didn't really understand what had happened or how, but I liked it. I held her, and she held me in a way no one else ever had. I never wanted to get out of bed; I wanted to freeze time in that moment.

"Do you want some coffee?" Keshani asked.

"Sure," I said, surprised at my own answer.

Normally, I'd want to get away as quickly as possible in situations like this. I had nothing to offer a woman and wanted nothing in return. But it felt different with Keshani. I never wanted to leave.

I lay in bed, trying to figure out what had happened and how I had ended up in her bed. She came in with two cups of coffee and handed me one. Daylight seeped through the curtains, illuminating the room in a suggestive way. As if the moment carried something that couldn't be easily brushed aside. She was so damn beautiful, sitting on the bed with her coffee cup in hand. Everything she did was perfect, and I felt like a filthy cockroach beside her. I couldn't help but stare at her, but I noticed she didn't appreciate it, so I tried to stop.

"You've slept with Rachel, haven't you?" Keshani said.

"A handful of times, but that was long ago," I said.

"Long ago..." Keshani said.

I wanted to say that Rachel didn't mean anything and that I already loved Keshani, that I wanted to grow old with her. But that would have been awkward, so I obviously said nothing. Keshani would break me one day. I knew that right away. She would kill me. And I intended to let her.

This is what I'll remember when she leaves me. That time she took the cucumber off my sandwich to add a slice of cheese. That memory will kill me over and over again. And I'll remember how she laughed, how her smile showed all of her teeth, and I'll remember everything about it. I'll lie in bed, tormented, as the light pierces through the blinds. It'll be so beautiful, the way the sun shines on my bedroom floor, even though I don't want it. And I'll hate that light because she won't be there to see it with me.

And hey, don't say I didn't warn you. You should've read that damn book about Zen and motorcycles instead.

Milton Keynes UK
Ingram Content Group UK Ltd.
UKHW040835021124
450589UK00001B/35